An unbelievable discovery...

Corwin blinked his eyes open. And gasped. There before him was the grandest sight he'd ever beheld. A crystal dome, higher than any mountain he'd seen or heard of, rose high into the sea. Blue-green lights blazed from within it, shining like the brightest stars. Delicate towers rose beneath the crystal dome, glimmering and shimmering in the light as if they'd been carved from pearls and opals.

This was more wondrous than the fairyland of legends. And Corwin could tell, from what he knew of the towers' height from Nia's memories, that the dome was still a couple of miles away.

"That's Atlantis?" he breathed.

Nia nodded. "Yes, it is."

Enjoy all three books in the *Water* Trilogy:

Water
BOOK THREE

TRANSFORMATION

KARA DALKEY

AVON BOOKS
An Imprint of HarperCollinsPublishers

For information address
HarperCollins Children's Books, a division of
HarperCollins Publishers, 1350 Avenue of the Americas,
New York, NY 10019.

 Produced by 17th Street Productions,
an Alloy, Inc. company
151 West 26th Street, New York, NY 10001

Library of Congress Catalog Card Number: 2001118043
ISBN 0-06-440810-8

First Avon edition, 2002

AVON TRADEMARK REG. U.S. PAT. OFF.
AND IN OTHER COUNTRIES,
MARCA REGISTRADA, HECHO EN U.S.A.

Visit us on the World Wide Web!
www.harperteen.com

Chapter One

"Is this going to hurt?" Corwin asked with more than a little trepidation. The warmth of the late summer sun beat down on his bare shoulders, but he was still shivering—and not just from the chilly seawater of Carmarthen Bay swirling below his waist.

"I don't know," Nia replied, a hint of concern in her aquamarine eyes. She brushed back a long strand of pale, silvery hair from her face. "I've never tried this kind of transformation."

That's not very encouraging, Corwin thought. "Because I remember watching your evil mermyd king Ma'el transform his fish tail into two legs," he said, "and he screamed a lot."

Nia glanced away a moment. "Yes, well, that was a bigger change than what Gobaith and I have planned for you."

"Ma'el is a lot more powerful than you and Gobaith.

And he still screamed," Corwin pointed out.

Nia sighed. "We're only going to help your gills to show themselves. And change your lungs a little. And give you webbing on your hands and feet, if you want."

"So basically, you're going to turn me into a frog," Corwin said, only half joking. "I've heard witches do that, you know."

Nia curved her arm under the water and sent a huge splash over him. "I'm not a witch! And you'll be a mermyd, not a frog. Whatever a *frog* is."

"Remind me to show you one someday." The cool sea spray felt good on Corwin's shoulders, and he couldn't help noticing that Nia looked very pretty when she was annoyed. But he wasn't really getting any more relaxed about all of this. He was terrified that the body he'd lived in—quite well, thank you—for the first sixteen years of his existence was about to be changed. Yes, he trusted Nia with his life. He was telepathically joined to her and had been for the three weeks since she had arrived on the shores of Wales. How could he not have grown to trust her? And he also trusted Gobaith, of course, the strange squidlike creature whose forebears had come from another world among the stars and who was also mentally joined to him and had magical power

Corwin would have once thought was unimaginable. But Corwin was still scared out of his mind. He wasn't about to show them just how scared, though.

He heard a bubbling in the water beside him. Gobaith had surfaced, his round, blobby head bobbing on the water, his saucer-sized golden eyes staring at Corwin.

Don't be afraid, Gobaith "said" in Corwin's mind. *This will be easy.*

So much for hiding my feelings, Corwin thought. It was possible, with a certain kind of concentration, to keep Nia or Gobaith from knowing his emotions. But it didn't always work. "I didn't ask if it would be hard, Gobaith. I asked if it would hurt."

Nia frowned at him. "What's a little pain to you? You said your late guardian Fenwyck used to hit you all the time. You survived that, didn't you?"

"That was different," Corwin grumbled. The bruises, cuts and welts Fenwyck had delivered had healed quickly enough and Corwin was himself again afterward. These changes might stay with him forever. Would he even know who he was anymore? Well, really, did he know now?

Most of his life, Corwin had been just a thief and

county fair charlatan, helping Fenwyck do cheap "magic" tricks for the crowd. Then Fenwyck had gotten himself killed after trying to steal a silver chalice from King Vortigern, and Corwin had had to hide out from the Royal Guard. Corwin had almost gotten used to being a poor beachcomber when he had happened upon the shell that had contained Gobaith, and then Nia had entered his life. Nothing had been the same after that. Even what he knew of his identity had been shattered when Gobaith had informed him that the father he'd never known had been a mermyd and that Corwin was part mermyd himself.

Nia, as she so often did, seemed to catch his thoughts. "Once you were a small boy. And now you're an older, taller boy. You'll never be that little boy again. Your body has already changed forever. And you won't stay as you are now forever, no matter what. Some day you'll get old and—"

"All right! All right!" Corwin surrendered. "I didn't say I was being reasonable."

That's good, Gobaith thought. *Because you aren't*.

Nia put her hand on Corwin's arm. "If we don't change you, you can't come with me to Atlantis to search for the sword we need to defeat Ma'el. Gobaith and I would have to leave you behind."

Corwin swallowed hard. She had touched on the one thing that bothered him more than pain and change. After the closeness he'd grown used to with Nia and Gobaith, being so distant from them would be almost unbearable. Especially since they had a dangerous and important duty ahead of them.

Ma'el had killed the reigning Farworlder kings of Atlantis to get their oculae, the walnut-sized organs in their foreheads that gave them magical abilities. By implanting these oculae into his body, Ma'el had gained their power. Ma'el, along with Joab, the Farworlder he was mentally joined to, had taken over Atlantis and had plans to conquer the "dry-lander" kingdoms as well. Corwin, Nia and Gobaith had been able to stop him once. But they couldn't completely defeat him. Not yet.

Nia was pretty sure she knew how, though. She had told him about a sword forged in Atlantis that had a special name, *Eikis Calli Werr*. The sword was said to have an oculus in its hilt that gave it special powers. Eikis Calli Werr had been meant to be a gift to the first dry-lander king who could bring peace to the world. Instead, it had sunk with Atlantis long ago, when Atlantis had fled the warmongering dry-land kingdoms. And now it had to be used in war, because it was the one hope Nia, Corwin and Gobaith had of defeating Ma'el and Joab. *If* they could find it.

"Are you sure you even know where this sword is?" Corwin asked, trying to give himself more time to gather his courage.

Nia sighed. "Well, it didn't come to these shores with my grand . . . with my father and me. So it must still be in the filtration tube where I last saw it. Or just outside of the tube hatch. If someone else hasn't found it first."

"What's a filtration tube?" Corwin asked, aware that he was grasping now.

"It's how Atlantis cleans its water." Suddenly Nia scowled and folded her arms across her chest. "You're stalling. Ma'el could be searching for the sword right now, and you're holding us up because of a little fear."

Corwin stood a bit straighter, his cheeks flushing. "That's not true. I just wanted to make sure . . . that we have a plan."

"We?"

"Yes. What?"

"Does that mean you're ready to make the transformation?"

"Of course," Corwin said with a bravado he only wished

he felt. "I couldn't just let you two swim off by yourselves. Imagine all the trouble you would get into without me there to pull you out!"

"Exactly," Nia said with a knowing smile. She placed her hands at the sides of his neck and closed her eyes.

Corwin let his eyes shut too and felt a searing pain as muscle tissue disconnected, reconnected, reformed and reshaped itself. *I can do this, I can do this,* he repeated to himself as he balled his hands into fists.

Corwin felt Gobaith touch his mind, soothing him, taking away the pain, until all Corwin could feel was some discomfort and tightness around his throat.

"There," Nia finally announced. "It's finished." She removed her hands from his neck.

Corwin reached up to feel what she'd done. Below his jawline, on either side of his neck, were three rows of new flaps of skin. They felt sort of like the shelflike mushrooms that grew on the sides of certain tree trunks. "How come my gills aren't lacy and delicate like yours?" he asked.

"Every mermyd's gills are different," Nia said with a shrug.

"Can I breathe with these now?" Corwin tried sucking

in air, but it took effort to keep the gill slits open as he breathed. Instead, he ended up gawping like a fish.

"The gills aren't made for air-breathing, silly," Nia teased. "They won't do much on land."

"Oh, right," Corwin said, wondering when he would ever stop embarrassing himself in front of her.

"Do you want me to try the webbing between your fingers now?" she asked.

"No, actually, um . . ." He trailed off. "I think I'll be able to swim just fine without that."

"You'll swim slower," she warned.

"Well, we're not running any races, are we?"

Nia's face became very serious. "We're in a race against Ma'el," she said. "The longer we let him recover, the more powerful he will become, and the more time he has to do damage to my people—if he hasn't already completely destroyed them."

Corwin bowed his head, feeling like a real fool. Since getting to know Nia and seeing Atlantis through her thoughts, he'd gotten to know her people. And now that he knew he was part mermyd himself, he understood that the Atlanteans were really his people as well. "I'm sorry. You're right. I guess I'm trying not to think about that."

"We *have* to think about it," Nia said. "At least *I* have to," she added, "since I'm the one who caused all their pain. I have to do what I can to set things right. Or die trying."

Corwin wanted to argue, as he often had in the past two weeks, to try to convince Nia that Ma'el's sabotage wasn't her fault. She shouldn't blame herself that Ma'el used her—tricked her into helping him kill the Farworlder kings of Atlantis. But Corwin knew the argument was useless. Nia felt responsible and that was that. "Other than that last part about dying, I . . . understand. Let me try breathing with these things now. The sooner we know I can use them, the sooner we can go." Corwin instinctively took a deep breath through his mouth and dove underwater. He breathed out. He breathed in—

And came up choking, sputtering, coughing. Corwin waded back to the rocky shore and draped himself over a boulder as he gasped, "The gills aren't working!"

Nia waded up to him. "Silly, you can't breathe in through *both* your mouth and your gills. I'm sorry, I should have warned you. I can see that this is going to take some practice."

Let me help you, Gobaith thought.

Corwin felt mixed emotions. Gobaith was still less than one year old, according to Nia, and Corwin could remember how childlike Gobaith's thoughts had been only three weeks ago. Even though Gobaith had grown and matured amazingly since then, it would take a lot of trust on Corwin's part to put Gobaith in charge of keeping him from drowning. But what choice did he have?

"Okay," Corwin agreed, tentatively. "What should I do?"

Come stand in this deeper water.

Taking a few deep breaths to make sure his lungs were now working properly again, Corwin waded out to where Gobaith floated, waiting for him. "Here I am, little squid. Now what?"

Just stand still. And before Corwin could say anything, Gobaith threw his smooth tentacles over Corwin's shoulders and crawled and slithered up his back.

"Hey! Hey! What are you doing?" It felt to Corwin like ten cold, clammy snakes were wrapping themselves around him.

Gobaith settled himself between Corwin's shoulder blades, tentacles wrapping around the boy's arms and waist. *Just getting comfortable. When you are ready, sit down in the water*.

"All right . . ."

One more thing—One of Gobaith's tentacles disengaged from Corwin's arm and wrapped itself around his head, firmly closing over his nose and mouth. *Now sit.*

"Mmmmph!" Corwin managed to get out, but he knew Gobaith wouldn't let go until he had tried to breathe with the gills. So he lifted his legs and let himself sink below the surface. With Gobaith's weight on top of him, Corwin quickly fell to the bottom.

For a few moments, panic made Corwin's heart race, and he was afraid he would suffocate at any moment. His gills flapped furiously, fluttering with fear. Moments passed, and moments passed. And then he was breathing. Not the sort of breathing he was used to, but his lungs were moving in and out, and he no longer felt the desperate need to surface.

A curious silvery fish with stripes on its sides swam up. It gave Corwin and Gobaith a dubious stare and then dashed away. Corwin became aware of a number of creatures underwater. Crabs crawling among the rocks; flower-like sea anemones; eels poking their heads out from crevices; an otter searching for a juicy clam; a seal chasing a school of tiny fish. It was all so amazing, Corwin didn't think about breathing at all.

I think he's ready, Gobaith sent. Gently, carefully, the tentacles around Corwin's face loosened and Gobaith swam aside.

Nia swam down to him, her hair streaming behind her like a long, silvery banner. "How do you feel?" she asked, bubbles streaming up from her mouth.

Corwin thought very hard before he answered—not about how he felt, but about how he could speak without mouth-breathing.

In through the gills, out through the mouth.

Corwin tried it. "I . . . feel . . . fine!" He laughed at the bubbles tickling his lips and nose. "This is great!"

Nia smiled. She was as beautiful underwater as she was on land. Maybe even more beautiful, if that were possible. "Good. Then we should get started."

"Wait! Shouldn't we take . . . something with us?"

Nia tilted her head as her hands and arms gently fanned the water. "Like what?"

"I don't know . . . food, a weapon? Water?"

Nia laughed out loud, arching her back. "Water? Water's everywhere!"

Corwin frowned. "I *did* notice that, but I can't drink seawater."

Nia became more serious. "As a mermyd, you'll see that you don't need fresh water."

"I'm only *part* mermyd," he reminded her. "What if it's not the part that needs fresh water?"

A strange expression came over her face. "Being only part mermyd shouldn't be a problem," she said. "And besides, Gobaith and I will make sure you're fine. As for food, the sea is full of it. We can catch it as we go—but I hope we won't take long getting back to Atlantis. We shouldn't need many meals. And most land weapons are useless underwater."

Corwin still felt unprepared, but he could feel Nia's urgency. And he was also genuinely eager to see Atlantis, not through Nia's eyes but through his own. "Okay. Let's go and give Ma'el another thrashing. Maybe he'll be so scared to see me coming that he'll just run, like King Vortigern did."

Nia smiled again, only this time it was like the sun coming out after many dreary days of rain. "Yes. Let's go."

Corwin waded back to shore to gather the few belongings that were important to him—a threadbare tunic and his knife. It was a plain, ordinary short dagger, but it was good for prying open clamshells.

Nag, the raven who had been Fenwyck's familiar, was perched on a nearby rock, pecking at a stubborn mussel. "Well, old bird," Corwin said. "I guess this is good-bye. Or maybe, even, farewell."

Nag looked up and tilted his head, as if to say, "So?"

Corwin scowled. "Oh, why do I expect you to actually care? You never liked me, did you? You just saved Gobaith from the kraken as a lark, right?" Despite his tone, Corwin couldn't bring himself to hate the bird anymore. Nag *had* saved Gobaith's life, and he'd been a big help during all of their recent ordeals.

"Raaaawk!" Nag cried, ruffling his feathers as if irritated and insulted.

"All right, all right, I'm sorry. But do you think you could do me one more favor? Could you go and say good-bye to the old blind button-maker, Henwyneb, for me? No, I guess that's asking a lot, even of a raven as smart as you."

Nag tilted his head again to regard Corwin a moment with the other eye. The bird clacked his beak, uttering something like, "Merk, merk," and then he suddenly flew off. Strangely enough, Nag was heading in the direction of Henwyneb's hut.

Corwin shook his head, put his knife in his trouser pocket and slipped his tunic over his head. Then, with a last look at the shores of Carmarthen Bay, he dove back into the sea.

*   *   *

At last, Nia thought as Corwin swam up beside her. She had been only vaguely aware of how anxious she'd become over the last several days, wanting to be on her way home. Even if home was now a ruin, it was where she belonged. She felt a little guilty bringing Corwin along—there would be so much he needed to learn. But Corwin, in his own cocky way, had been right. She and Gobaith needed him, needed his magic power and strength and quick wits, if they were to have any chance of defeating Ma'el once and for all.

A small part of her heart was glad that Corwin was coming along for another reason, but Nia didn't want to think about that. Until she had done her duty to help Atlantis, she couldn't allow her emotions to be distracted.

Gobaith did happy somersaults in the water ahead of her, tentacles streaming behind him. Nia was amazed at how much he had grown in just a few weeks. Once he could fit snugly in the palm of her hand, but now he was two-thirds as long as she was tall. Pretty soon he'd be bigger than she was, possibly even bigger than Corwin if his current growth was any guide.

With Corwin at her side, Nia turned and swam out toward the open sea. It was hard not to be distracted by the many, many creatures that lived in these shallower waters—creatures Nia had learned about in Academy but had never actually seen.

A playful seal swam alongside Gobaith and did barrel-rolls in the water with him before dashing off again. A small pod of dolphins approached, gray with darker gray lines along the side as well as a yellow streak from eye to tail. Suddenly Nia, Corwin and Gobaith were in the middle of them, a couple of dolphins above, two below and one to either side. Nia squeaked at them in a way that would be a friendly greeting to the Atlantean dolphins she knew. These dolphins didn't seem to speak the same "language," but they did act sociable. The ones to either side kept gently nudging Corwin and Nia, daring them to swim faster.

Only Gobaith took the bait, and he sped ahead. Squealing with anticipation of the race, the whole pod took off after him. Nia vaguely remembered something about how dolphins sometimes eat squid, and she sent the thought to Gobaith, *Be careful!*

Corwin laughed beside her. A land-dweller's laugh underwater was a strange sound. "I don't think we'll have to worry about Gobaith. Look at him go!"

The Farworlder led the dolphins on a merry chase,

circling over and under Corwin and Nia, staying just ahead of the lead dolphin, even leaping out of the water.

"I hope he doesn't wear himself out," Nia said, but she was enjoying the show, too.

Suddenly Corwin tensed beside her. "Nia, watch out!" Corwin's knife was in his hand. Nia looked to her right. A huge conical shape was approaching—a giant gray mouth agape with eyes atop it and a shark's body behind.

Nia paused and began to gather her power to fend it off, but the shark turned aside, avoiding them. Nia sighed in a cloud of bubbles when she realized what it was. "It's all right, Corwin. I've heard of those creatures—it's a basking shark. It only eats tiny animals, the sort of things that make up the kraken. It won't eat anything bigger, especially not us."

"If that thing eats kraken, then more power to it. Good shark, I say. Good boy!"

Nia laughed. "No, it doesn't eat kraken, just—oh, never mind. Where did Gobaith go?"

I'm over here. Off in the murky distance, Nia saw a waving tentacle. "Please don't get too far ahead, Gobaith!"

"Now you know how I felt in the cistern below Vortigern's castle," Corwin muttered, behind her.

Nia turned. "One thing I should have warned you about. Sound carries very far in water. If you don't want me to hear you say something, you'll have to say it in sign language."

"Why would that matter?" Corwin asked. "You'll hear me think it, won't you?"

"Maybe, although if you concentrate on directing a thought just at Gobaith, I might not catch it. Of course, I'll feel slightly hurt and left out if I know you've done that," Nia said with a toss of her head. She turned and continued swimming on.

Nia didn't know what to do about Corwin's ambivalence toward the telepathic joining. Even though it had been weeks since both she and Corwin had been "marked" by Gobaith, Corwin still fought to hide his thoughts from both of them, only letting them in now and then. Nia suspected why Corwin kept her out, but Gobaith couldn't understand and was confused by it. Atlanteans were taught from an early age that joining with a Farworlder was the greatest honor a mermyd could experience and that it was only beneficial. Corwin, however, was still terrified by it.

Corwin has so many fears, and he works so hard to not let us see them, Nia thought. *Doesn't he know that the bravest ones aren't those who have no fear, but those who overcome their fears? He probably wouldn't believe me if I told him that.*

He is young. He will learn, Gobaith thought at her, clearly shielding *that* thought from Corwin.

You should talk, little one, Nia thought back.

Yes, but I learn faster.

They swam for hours as the water got colder and colder. Nia tried to reach out with her mind and heart for Atlantis, trying to sense it within the unis. But she could only determine that it was in a southwesterly direction. She couldn't tell how far or how deep. *Where is it? It can't be far if I reached Corwin's land soon after leaving.* Nia allowed herself to surface, Corwin popping up beside her, to see how far they'd gone. The shores they had left were still a greenish-brown line on the northeastern horizon.

Out here, the water wasn't calm as it had been in the bay. White-crested sea swells rose high, lifting Nia and Corwin up and dropping them down. It was dizzying, disorienting, and so Nia dove back into the calmer depths. Corwin reluctantly followed.

"So how far is it?" Corwin asked.

"I don't know," Nia admitted.

"YOU DON'T KNOW?"

"You don't have to shout," she snapped. "I told you, sound carries underwater. I was unconscious when I woke up in your land, so I don't know how I got there from Atlantis. I only know it's this way." Actually, Nia was beginning to worry about her inability to sense the way home. She'd always assumed she could find it, the way so many fish can find the place they were born, without even thinking.

Gobaith swam over to her and gently wrapped a tentacle around her wrist. *Don't blame yourself. My fathers and mothers and ancestors have all worked to keep the city hidden within the unis. They have cast spells to hide its location and to prevent outsiders from reaching it. We couldn't simply swim to it, even if we knew its physical location. You and I reached Corwin's land, Nia, because Ar'an carried us there. He used the last of his powers to bend the unis, to place us on that shore.*

"Oh," Nia said, surprised, but even more discouraged. "Did he choose our landing because Corwin was there?"

Perhaps. I think Ar'an sensed a beacon of power in Corwin's land. I sense it too, but I don't know what it is. Our kind visited that land, long, long ago, but that is all the unis tells me.

"We found a ruin that had Atlantean writing in it, while we were on our way to Vortigern's castle," Corwin jumped in.

That may be where the beacon is, then.

"But what are we going to do?" Nia asked.

"Yes," Corwin agreed. "Why did we swim out all this way if we can't even hope to get where we're going?"

Patience, my friends. I'm leading us to a particular place. I found the knowledge within Nia's mind, though she herself doesn't remember it.

"Remember what?" Nia asked.

The transfer points. You were taught about them in an ancient history lecture at the Academy a year ago. You might have remembered better, except your mind kept wandering to thoughts of a certain attractive male mermyd who was—

"Forget about that!" Nia blurted, blushing as she remembered the day when she had first noticed Cephan. What a mistake that had been. "What about the transfer points?"

My forebears had hoped that, in time, peaceful land-dweller kingdoms would spread around this entire planet. They had wanted a way to travel swiftly, to be prepared for the time when land-dwellers were ready to accept Farworlders and the knowledge we have to offer. Unfortunately, that was not to be once Atlantis had to hide beneath the waves. But a few transfer points had already been built, and one of them is nearby. My oculus can sense its faint signal.

"But how will *we* use the transfer point?" Corwin asked.

The same way my ancestors planned. We will use its energy to enhance our magic, with which we will fold the unis.

"Fold it?" Corwin persisted, "like . . . cloth?"

Exactly. The edges of a piece of cloth may be far apart when it's flat, but if the cloth is folded, the edges can be right together. By folding the fabric of space and time, relative to ourselves, two locations that may be far apart will seem side by side, and it will take no time to get there.

Nia found it difficult to fold her own mind around the idea, but she trusted Gobaith. Every passing day, she was amazed at the growing wisdom and confidence the young Farworlder displayed. Still, one thought concerned her. "If the transfer point sends a signal to your oculus, then Ma'el and Joab can find it too."

We can only hope they haven't bothered to look for it yet.

"Then we'd better hurry," Nia said. "Lead on, Gobaith."

The Farworlder led them down and down, deeper into the sea. The water became even colder, and Nia liked it. After all, it was what she had been used to in Atlantis. She could tell, however, that Corwin was becoming uncomfortable.

"You can use our magical power to warm yourself a little," she suggested to him, "so that you can adjust to the cold more gradually."

"I don't want to waste any," Corwin said, though his teeth were chattering. "We don't know how much energy we're going to need at the transfer point."

"True," Nia said, "but we don't want your mind too numbed from cold when we get there."

"I'll be fine," Corwin growled.

A low moaning came rumbling through the water, reverberating against their skin.

"What was *that?*" Corwin shouted, looking wildly around.

"It's a whale song," Nia said, smiling with wonder.

She paused to drift and listen. "I had heard that the humpbacks are the greatest singers in the world. Now I know that it's true."

"That's *singing?*"

"Sssh." Nia tilted her head back and tried to interpret the high squeals and low booms of the songs, but she didn't know the humpbacks' "language." She could see them now—dark shapes, like moving mountains, swimming in the distance.

They're calling to other whale families far away, Gobaith interpreted. *They're telling each other where to find the best feeding places.*

"Amazing that simple conversation can sound so beautiful," Nia breathed.

Wait, Gobaith thought, and Nia sensed a new urgency coming from him. *The nearest family is saying they sense something strange in the water. There are predators approaching. They're going to leave for safer waters.*

"Predators? Do they mean us? Or a land-dweller ship?"

No, not us. I, too, sense something isn't right.

Nia looked around. A pod of three sleek black-and-white orcas was approaching. Nia admired them, too, for a moment, then noticed that the orcas were headed in their direction in a very determined fashion.

Help me create a shield, both of you.

"But Gobaith—"

Just do it!

Trusting the Farworlder's instincts, Nia brought her arms up crossed in front of her. With Gobaith feeding her energy, she helped him thicken the water ahead into a spherical, transparent wall surrounding them.

The orcas slid along the wall, mouths gaping wide, displaying tooth-lined jaws. They circled the transparent wall as if looking for a way in.

"Aren't these what fishermen call killer whales?" Corwin asked.

"That's an unfair name," Nia said, still shocked at what she was seeing. "Orcas do not attack mermyds or land-dwellers. And they're smart—but not this smart." Nia kicked her legs and turned in place, trying to keep the wall strongest next to where the orcas were swimming.

And these have brought friends.

"Sharks!" Corwin cried.

Pale as death, three white sharks swam into view. These were also coming straight at Nia, Gobaith and Corwin. Upon reaching the protective sphere, the sharks began circling with the orcas.

"Won't making this water wall use up the power we'll need to get us to Atlantis?" Corwin asked.

We will never reach Atlantis if we die first.

"Good point."

"I'm sure that's what Ma'el is counting on," Nia said. "This has to be coming from him. Those sharks don't even belong in these waters. And they aren't even trying to attack yet. They're just hoping to wear us down."

Yes, sent Gobaith. *I can sense Ma'el's power in this*.

More dark shapes joined the orcas and the white sharks—sharks of every length and description, spotted and striped, large and small. They joined the other sharks, circling, watching and waiting.

The hair on Nia's neck stood on end as she watched the eerie parade of predators. She shivered, the chilly water finally getting to her. She could feel her arms tiring, and there was a growing hollowness in her stomach as she imagined what the sharks would do if—or when—the wall failed. She, Corwin and Gobaith could have used their magic to fight off as many as three or four sharks, maybe. But these were too many. Far too many. Nia clenched her fists and her jaw and tried to keep her courage up.

"We've got to do *something*," Corwin said. "If we just

stay like this, we won't have a chance. Gobaith, could you open a small space in the wall? Maybe I could kill them one at a time."

"That might work with the small sharks," Nia said, "but the orcas could swallow you whole before you even touched them."

"Great," he muttered.

Nia could feel the hunger of the sharks and orcas building. She didn't know if that was Ma'el's work or if they simply hadn't eaten since they were summoned here. Once either she or Corwin or Gobaith were even wounded, there would be a feeding frenzy the likes of which these waters hadn't seen before.

Nia's heart thudded in her chest and her gills worked furiously. The magical wall was cutting off water flow, making it harder and harder to draw oxygen from it. They had even less time than she'd imagined. She and Corwin would suffocate before the spell wore out. *There's no way the three of us can defeat so many of them*, she thought sadly. *If only we had our own army to fight them. Or if only* . . . "Wait!" she said suddenly. "I have an idea. . . ."

Chapter Two

"Tell us your idea!" Corwin demanded, his gills flapping furiously. "I'm running out of air! Is that part of Ma'el's battle plan, too?" Corwin turned round and round in the small magical sphere. The circling sharks and orcas, their sharp teeth gleaming, were making him terrified, not to mention dizzy. He tried not to bump into Gobaith, who floated in the center of the sphere, his ten tentacles standing straight out like a hedgehog's quills, sending energy to the sphere wall.

"We need moving water to breathe," Nia answered. "This protective bubble we've built has made the water inside too still. There's no fresh oxygen getting in, and we're using up what little there is. But listen—if Gobaith and I can make a little hole in this wall, just big enough for your knife, and you can stab just one of the sharks, they're so hungry that the scent of blood in the water will cause them to kill and eat each other."

"They will?" Corwin asked. "You're sure?"

"Yes."

"But I have to reach my hand through the wall?"

"Not far, just enough to stab one when it swims near. It's better than letting them in with us, even one at a time, isn't it?"

Corwin couldn't argue with that. "But what if Ma'el can keep them from going mad at the scent of blood?"

"I get the feeling he's barely holding them in check," Nia said. "Controlling so many animals would be hard, even for Ma'el. Besides, it's not like we have any other options right now."

"Gobaith, what do you think?" Corwin asked. "Should we do it?"

It will be difficult. You will have to be careful to stab at the right time. But they are circling close to the wall. It's worth trying. Nia, I'm going to make an opening near Corwin. Try to keep the water wall firm around it so that I don't "pop" our bubble.

Nia nodded and turned to face the sphere wall beside Corwin. A bright vertical line appeared in the sphere to Corwin's right. The line broadened until it was the width of his hand. *There it is. Hurry.*

Corwin swam up right beside the wall, his knife gripped

in his hand. He waited until a white shark swam very close. As soon as the head passed by, Corwin stabbed out with the knife, scoring a cut along the shark's right fin. The shark turned, as if to bite, but it bumped its head into the wall. It continued to swim in a circle with the others, but in a wobbly manner, leaving a thin stream of blood behind it.

That's good. I feel their anxiety, but Ma'el's controlling spell still holds. You will need to wound more of them.

"It's never as easy as it sounds, is it?" Corwin muttered, as he positioned himself, arm cocked back, beside Gobaith's hole in the wall. Another shark swam close: a large spotted one. Corwin stabbed, but only scratched its side.

"Keep trying," Nia urged. She was beginning to look a little drawn and pale from the effort of keeping the hole contained and the wall solid.

Corwin positioned himself again and waited. He felt himself weakening from the lack of oxygen in the water. He began to wonder if the spots he was seeing were the sharks or some sign of suffocation.

Then a little shark, only three feet long, came swimming sideways along the wall, belly facing Corwin. *Now's my best chance.* Closer, closer, the shark wriggled, and then Corwin punched the knife through the hole as hard as he could. The shark struggled to free itself, opening the wound wider and longer down its belly.

"Bring your hand back, Corwin, quick!" Nia cried.

Corwin jerked his hand back as a cloud of shark blood bloomed before him. The dying shark flailed helplessly, unable to swim with the others.

The little shark's death throes were too enticing for the ravenous, circling predators. A great white swam up and bit the small shark in half. A gray mako shark attacked the white to snatch the morsel away, leaving a bloody scar on the white's snout. An orca rushed the white shark and bit its head off.

After that, everything was a terrifying blur. Corwin huddled with Nia and Gobaith as writhing bodies bit and slashed each other just beyond the water wall. The orcas tore the large sharks to pieces, shaking their gigantic heads to make the prey in their jaws fall to pieces. The large sharks gobbled the small ones in one or two bites and then fought each other over the scraps.

Corwin could feel the sheer strength of the orcas as they slammed up against the magical bubble wall. It was a good thing that most of the violence was hidden in a dark cloud of blood. Corwin already knew he wasn't going to want to eat again for a while.

And then it was over. The only survivors, to no one's surprise, were the orcas. Their hunger fully sated, they swam away, leaving Corwin, Nia and Gobaith in the midst of a mess of shark soup.

"I know we need fresh water to breathe," Nia said softly, "but is it possible we could find better water than this before we let down our wall, Gobaith?"

"Yes," Corwin agreed. "I'd rather not be picking shark bones out of my shiny new gills." Nor did he have any wish to taste the water just outside the sphere.

Help me swim, and we can get some distance from this, Gobaith sent, *but it will weaken us further*.

"I don't think we'll have to go far," Corwin said.

"No, the . . . remains would take time to spread in the sea," Nia said. "And we don't want to stay here long anyway. Other predators will want to come scavenging what's left of the sharks." She put her arm around Gobaith, between his head and his tentacles, and motioned for Corwin to do the same.

Corwin hesitated. He had rarely touched the Farworlder. He wondered if Gobaith was slimy. But Corwin swam up to the other side of Gobaith and put his arm around the Farworlder, next to Nia's. Gobaith's skin was slightly warm and smooth, not at all what Corwin had expected. Corwin and Nia began kicking gently, moving the three of them slowly, and the bubble wall followed with them.

Luckily, as Nia predicted, they didn't have to swim very far to find cleaner water. *Good,* Gobaith sent. *We can let down the wall now.* The Farworlder and Nia both drooped, exhausted from holding up the sphere.

Cold, fresh seawater flowed around them. Corwin was amazed how much it was like a breath of fresh air through his gills. The three of them rolled lazily in the water for a bit, just to regather their strength.

Finally Corwin had recovered enough. Enough to realize the disturbing implications of what they'd just been through. "If that was a trap Ma'el set for us, how did he know exactly where to find us?" he asked. "This is a big ocean."

Nia frowned. "He must have seen through the unis that we were coming this way."

Or he's watching us, Gobaith offered.

Corwin looked around, but it was hard to make out anything in the murky depths besides the shimmer of distant schools of fish. "Do you think he's nearby?"

"He doesn't have to be," Nia said. "He can probably use all sorts of sea creatures as his spies. Especially if he can control them like the orcas and sharks."

"So you're saying he could ambush us again at any time?" Corwin asked, his whole body chilling at the thought.

"I'm afraid so," Nia said. "Gobaith, could you possibly see ahead enough in the unis to tell us when Ma'el will attack again?"

Gobaith emitted his strange, bubbling laughter. *That wouldn't be possible. It's easy for Ma'el to disguise his intentions in ways that I can't untangle. Even now, as I probe the unis with my thoughts, I can only see that there will be trouble ahead, but I can't tell where, when or what it will be.*

Corwin sighed, making a cloud of bubbles around his cheeks. "So much for the three of us being able to trip him up," he grumbled.

"We can't give up hope," Nia said firmly. "It won't be just the three of us once we find the sword. The oculus in Eikis Calli Werr's hilt will bind our power, hopefully in a way Ma'el and Joab can't defend against."

Suddenly a new worry struck Corwin. "What if Ma'el finds the sword first?" he asked.

"There's a good chance he doesn't know about its power," Nia replied. "My grand . . . my father told me about it privately. It's not common knowledge in Atlantis. Most people just think of the sword as a pretty land-dweller artifact brought out for ceremonies and parades."

Corwin's gut tightened as he had a sickening suspicion. "If Ma'el has spies listening to us, he just found out about the sword, didn't he? We just told him."

Nia glanced around nervously. "I hope not."

I don't think Ma'el has "ears" anywhere close to us, Gobaith thought in response. *But it's best to say little about the sword from now on. Ma'el is still afraid of us, or he wouldn't be setting traps. Therefore Nia is right. We shouldn't give up hope.*

"Can we set up some sort of . . . sensing field, so that we can tell when Ma'el's magic is at work in the area?" Nia asked.

Our strength is needed to get us to Atlantis, remember? If we waste it searching for danger that might not come, then we will never get home at all.

Nia sighed and shook her head. "Then I guess we just have to swim on blindly."

Corwin swam over to her and put his hand on her shoulder. "That's how we've been doing things all along, Nia. And we've survived this far, haven't we? In my experience, with all the visions I had when I was a boy, trying to know the future has never done me or anyone else any good. And maybe that's a good way to defeat Ma'el. If he doesn't know our defenses because *we* don't know our defenses, then he can't plan ahead to counter us."

Nia laughed. "I'm so glad you're with us, Corwin. You see the world so differently. You could find the smallest pearl in a colony of snapping oysters."

"My master Fenwyck always taught me to look for the easy money."

"That's not what I meant," Nia said with another chuckle, "but thanks anyway." She rested her head on his shoulder and let him hold her for a moment. No matter what dangers lay ahead, it made Corwin feel wonderful.

At last, self-consciously, Nia pulled away. With an embarrassed smile, she asked Gobaith, "Should we keep going now?"

I thought you'd never ask, Gobaith replied, but he wasn't disapproving. The Farworlder swam ahead, though not as quickly as he had before.

"If there aren't any more attacks, will we have enough energy to get us to Atlantis, Gobaith?"

I hope so.

As they swam farther and farther from land, and the coastal shelf below them slanted down and down, Nia began to have a sense of how wide and vast the open sea was. She remembered how she'd once had dreams of being a wild mermyd, of escaping the social confines of Atlantis and just swimming free. But now she saw how empty and lonely the ocean was, despite all the wondrous life that swam in it. She was glad she hadn't pursued that particular dream.

"Are we there yet?" Corwin asked. "I'm getting tired."

Not much farther, Gobaith sent.

Nia reached out with her senses and found the magnetic lines in the water and, more faintly, in the earth below. The lines were becoming a bit less parallel, a bit more chaotic. But many lines veered toward each other, converging toward a region just a league or two ahead. "There aren't as many fish here, or other sea life," Nia observed.

Wise animals would avoid this place—it would confuse and disorient them. We must take care not to become disoriented ourselves.

"You mean," Corwin began, "that the direction sense that I got from joining with you will go away now?"

Not go away, just become confused and unreliable.

"Oh. So I'll be back to normal, then. Part of me, anyway."

Nia laughed. But her smile quickly faded as the water around her began to feel unsettled. It was moving, like one of the aerating currents that flowed around the circumference of

Atlantis. It began to push her to the right, and it was picking up speed.

"Am I imagining it," Corwin asked, "or is there a reason I can't seem to swim straight?"

"It's real," Nia said, feeling the water carry her sideways. "Gobaith, is this part of the disorientation you talked about?"

I don't know . . . I . . . oh, no . . .

The water current flowed even faster, and now Nia could barely swim against it. It was just like the tunnels in Atlantis. Which meant that she and Corwin would soon not be able to breathe, unless they found something to hang onto.

With horrible, growing shock, Nia saw that a structure was forming in the vast region of water around them. It was similar to their magical wall, but enormous—reaching from the surface of the ocean far above, to the seabed far below.

"Maelstrom!" Corwin cried. "It's a giant whirlpool. Henwyneb once told me about these. Fishermen told him stories about how these could suck down whole ships that would never be seen again."

"Gobaith!" Nia shouted. "Is this caused by the transfer point?"

No! It's another trap set by Ma'el!

The water was swirling faster and faster, and Nia couldn't swim against it at all. By turning and tilting her head she could get some water flowing past her gills, but it took all her concentration.

A familiar red serpentine shape appeared in the middle of the whirlpool. "Of course," Corwin growled bitterly. "It's the kraken. Ma'el's favorite pet. Why am I not surprised?"

The kraken screamed, a sound that reverberated underwater, sending shivers through Nia's bones. "We've stopped the kraken many times before," Nia said, trying to keep her courage up. "I'm sure there's something we can do. Isn't there?"

"I need sunlight!" Corwin replied. "Only the sun stops it. There's no sunlight down here."

"Can't you summon sunlight like you did in King Vortigern's castle?"

"I made a burning glass between my hands that time. Even if I can get my hands into position, we're moving so fast I don't think I could aim at the kraken very well."

The false sunlight would be weakened by the water, Gobaith sent, *so such a spell may not be the best use of our energy.*

Nia saw Corwin moving his arms, trying to get them

into a position to do something. Apparently, the kraken saw it too, because it lunged toward Corwin. The kraken grew a scarlet tentacle out of its neck, and the new limb wrapped itself around Corwin, pinning his arms to his side. The kraken grew another two tentacles. It lunged across the whirlpool at Nia and wrapped its new limbs around her, one around her arms, the other around her mouth. At first she was afraid it might cover and hold down her gills, but the kraken let her breathe. *Of course,* she thought. *Ma'el wants us alive if he can manage it. Maybe we should just let the kraken take us to Atlantis.*

No! Gobaith sent to her, as a fourth appendage grew out of the kraken and wrapped itself around the Farworlder. *I have looked into the unis. We must not give Ma'el this chance to capture us!*

But we're as helpless as babies, Nia thought in despair. *What else can we do?*

Chapter Three

What can I do? What can I do? Corwin wondered. It was clear that the kraken wasn't going to swallow them whole this time, but the myriad little creatures that made up the tentacle around his chest and arms were itching his skin fiercely, as if they were nibbling at him. He wanted to scream, kick, do *something*. But he didn't have any clever ideas, and there were no pithy lessons from his late master Fenwyck that would apply to this situation at all. Fenwyck never talked about "when you're caught by monsters." Only about "when you're caught by angry shop owners."

Corwin needed sunlight to get the kraken to disintegrate, but daylight was impossibly far away. He looked up toward the ocean surface, where tiny glimmers of sunlight danced. Corwin didn't have nearly enough strength to swim up there, dragging Nia and Gobaith and the kraken with him. He'd have to be as big as the kraken itself to do that. *I don't think I can change shape that much.*

Nia seemed to be following his thoughts—she was also gazing up toward the surface. She looked at him as if to speak, but the kraken's tentacle was still over her mouth.

Then her thoughts came very clearly to his mind. *Corwin, your mouth is free. I want you to make this sound.* A noise followed that was a squeal descending into a mountainous moan—like the whale song they had heard earlier, only higher in pitch.

"I can't make that kind of noise," Corwin answered, baffled. "Why? What will it do?"

Try. Please.

I will help, Gobaith sent.

Corwin had no idea what Nia was up to. But he'd trusted her before and she'd saved his life. And at least it was something to do. He opened his mouth and did his best to perform the strange bellow. The sound he made was somewhere between a gargantuan belch and the scream of a frightened horse.

Very good. Do it again.

Corwin sighed. Gathering all the air he could through his gills, he did. This time the sound was more like the lowest note he could sing, sliding up to one of Nag's most annoying screeches. When finished, he shouted at Nia, "So what *is* that?"

It's the cry of an infant whale in distress, she responded.
"What possible good—"
JUST DO IT! AGAIN!

So Corwin continued to utter the noises, though his lungs and throat weren't used to such stress. Even yelling over the crowds at county fairs didn't take this much lung power and vocal range. He had the feeling Gobaith was assisting him, using his belly muscles to squeeze the lungs just so, helping him with mouth and tongue position. Corwin wondered if this call was meant to frighten the kraken or if it would bring back the sharks, looking for an easy meal. Would the sharks eat the kraken? Maybe the big basking sharks would. But the cry of an infant whale wouldn't interest basking sharks, would it?

The kraken was watching the entire time, as if fascinated with the noise. Corwin wondered if it was really Ma'el looking out through those strange, empty eyes, or if the kraken had some minuscule mind of its own. The kraken seemed to come to some decision, and it began to grow another scarlet tentacle—probably to shut Corwin up.

Suddenly, the water around them rumbled with a bone rattling, rolling bellow. A vast, dark shape cut through the swirling water below them as if the whirlpool were no impediment at all. As the thing swam by again, closer,

Corwin saw that it was a whale. But bigger than any whale he'd ever seen. It was bigger than any of the houses in Carmarthen. Its back was blue, only somewhat darker than the water around them.

Do the call one more time, Nia's thoughts came to Corwin.

"I was calling *that?*" Corwin asked in amazement. But he took one more deep breath and uttered the moaning squeal.

The great blue whale swam beneath them all, turning on its side to eye Corwin as it passed. It continued on without stopping. "I don't think it's convinced I'm a baby whale."

Just wait.

The whale had circled around and was coming back at them very fast. Corwin couldn't believe that anything that massive could move so swiftly. Before he had time for another thought, the whale's back rammed up into them. Corwin, Nia, Gobaith and the kraken were all being carried up and up on the whale's back. The kraken wriggled and writhed and shrieked in protest, but because of their speed, the water pressed down on them like a vice. They were all held firmly to the whale's back.

Let out your breath, Corwin! Nia commanded. *Don't hold air in your lungs. It could kill you.*

Corwin breathed out in a long stream of bubbles as the whale rose. *My own breath could kill me? The ocean sure is a strange place. There's so much I need to learn—if I survive long enough.*

With a last burst of speed, the blue whale breached the surface and arced up over the water. Corwin took a deep gasp of air and then smiled in the bright afternoon sunlight. Again, Corwin was amazed at the power and strength of the whale as almost all of its body came out of the water before the head splashed back down with a mighty crash. Two great walls of water were flung up on either side of its jaws. The whale blew steam and water out of a hole in its back, higher than any fountain Corwin had ever seen.

The kraken screamed, a chorus of millions of tiny mouths wailing, and then it exploded, covering all of them with its red liquid. Then it flowed off down the whale's corrugated back, turning into normal seawater as it returned to the ocean.

Corwin lay a moment on the whale's back, hoping the great blue wasn't planning on going anywhere right away. He needed a rest. Nia was studying the pattern of scars on the whale's thick hide.

"This is amazing!" she said. "This is the same whale

who would sing at events in Atlantis. Did Ma'el set you loose, old girl? How lucky for us! Corwin, this whale sang at the last Trials when my cousin . . . my cousin Garun . . ."

"Won the right to be Avatar," Corwin finished for her.

"Yes." Nia hung her head. "And the chance to be murdered by Ma'el and Cephan," she added, softly.

Corwin could feel the sorrow in her heart. "Garun was the one who should have been joined to Gobaith, not us."

"Yet here we are," Nia sighed.

It felt strange to be lying on the whale's back as though he were a seal basking on a rocky island. Looking around, Corwin noticed that there was no land in sight. "Where are we?" he asked. "How much farther is the transfer point to Atlantis? And how are we going to get there if Ma'el keeps setting traps for us? Hey—where did Gobaith go?"

I'm here. Gobaith's round head bobbed up out of the water beside the whale. *When the kraken exploded, it threw me a little ways away. I've never flown so high. I wish I had more time to study that so I could do it again*.

"You're still young, aren't you?" Corwin said fondly. "We *do* have more important things to think about right now."

It will be a while, Gobaith sent, *before Ma'el can unleash his next obstacle. It must have taken amazing power to summon the kraken and cause the whirlpool, at* such a distance from Atlantis. Ma'el will need time to recover his energy.

"But if it takes us time to reach the gate or whatever to get to Atlantis, Ma'el might have enough time to stop us again," Corwin complained. "He can rebuild the kraken as often as he wants."

The Farworlder scuttled up the whale's back. *Don't despair. The answer has found us.*

"What does *that* mean?" Corwin asked.

Our friend here, Gobaith tapped the whale, *knows the location of the transfer point. She can get us there much faster than we can swim.*

Corwin remembered the speed at which the whale could move. "Ummm . . . will that be safe?"

Safer than waiting for Ma'el to attack us again.

"Good point."

Gobaith slithered up to the whale's head, in front of its blowhole. He settled down, extending his tentacles out like the spokes of a cartwheel. Corwin could sense that Gobaith was somehow communicating with the whale the same way the Farworlder did with him and Nia, though it was requiring more effort.

Nia crawled up beside him. "We'd better hold on tight," she said. "When this old girl moves, she moves!"

"Yeah, I noticed that." Corwin copied the way Nia was grabbing onto the folds in the blue whale's skin.

"Now lie down this way," Nia instructed, stretching herself out parallel to the whale's body. "That way you won't get knocked off by the water."

"Whatever you say." Corwin stretched himself out lengthwise.

Suddenly the whale lurched forward and dove back into the water. Corwin cried out as the whale went almost vertical, head down, sinking beneath the waves. He held on with fingers and toes with all his might as the cold water of the North Atlantic again washed over him. Deeper and deeper the whale dove, at great speed, until Corwin had to shut his eyes and bury his face in the skin folds on the whale's back. The water moved past him at great speed, but instead of finding it hard to breathe, as he had in the whirlpool, Corwin found that the water shoving against his shoulders forced oxygenated water into his gills. He hardly had to work to breathe at all. It was exhilarating.

After the whale made what seemed like a wide curve to the left, Corwin could feel her powerful muscles undulate beneath him as she picked up even more speed. Nothing Corwin had ever known could move this fast: not even a horse. He dared to turn his head to look at Nia. She was smiling again, happy to at last be going home. Corwin looked ahead at Gobaith. The Farworlder had flattened himself against the whale's head, but with ten tentacles to hold on with, he was doing quite well. And Corwin got the distinct impression that Gobaith was thinking something like *wheeeeeeeeee!*

The blue whale finally slowed enough so that Nia could raise herself up on her elbows and look around. They were circling a structure that could only have been made by an ancient advanced civilization, like Atlantis. It consisted of several circles of standing stones topped with lintels, one ring within another. Each of the stones was covered with carvings, writing and petroglyphs. A huge purple crystal glowed at the center. A transparent, low dome of crystal formed a roof over it all.

The structure stood at the edge of the continental shelf—not far from its outermost ring, the sea floor fell away in an enormous cliff. Nia couldn't see the bottom of it in the darkness below.

"I've heard of a place like this in my country," Corwin said. "It's called Stonehenge, and the druids worship there."

"Maybe long ago some of your people learned about

the transfer points and tried to build one themselves," Nia suggested.

"Maybe. All I know is it's said to be older than anyone knows. This place is older than the Romans too, right?"

Nia laughed. "When Atlantis was above the surface, Rome was just a collection of villages and tribes with a central market. That's what they told me in Academy, anyway."

"Well, Rome's gotten a lot bigger since then."

"So I heard."

"You know," Corwin said, "it's strange how kingdoms rise in power, becoming so grand, and then just fall. I wonder what makes them strong and then weak. I wish I knew more about history."

Nia saw a hunger in Corwin's eyes that she hadn't seen before—a hunger for knowledge.

"If we succeed," she said, "I'll show you the Atlantean archives where all the records of the world's history are kept. At least, all the world that Atlantis knows."

"I would like that," he said.

The blue whale came to a stop and settled on the shelf floor beside the outermost stone ring of the structure.

She says we must get off now, Gobaith sent. *She has to return to the surface to breathe.*

"Tell her thanks, Gobaith," Nia said as she jumped off

the whale's back and swam aside. "She's very generous."

She asks only that we do all we can to defeat Ma'el. Gobaith launched himself off of the whale's head and came zooming through the water over to Nia.

"Well, that's the plan," Corwin said. He patted the whale's flank, saying, "Thanks, old girl," and also swam over to Nia.

The whale uttered a mountainous bellow of good-bye and good luck. She rose up majestically from the sea floor and with a massive wave of her tail, headed for the surface. The backwash from the wave sent Nia, Corwin and Gobaith gently colliding into the outermost ring of stones.

"Nia! Look at this!" Corwin exclaimed. "These carvings are just like those at the buried temple we found on our way to Castle Carmarthen. What do they mean?"

"I don't know, and we don't have time to study them right now. I think some of the writing is ancient land-dweller languages, too, but I can't be sure."

That will teach you not to daydream at Academy lectures, Gobaith sent.

"I promise, once we defeat Ma'el, I'll be the best student the Academy's ever seen," Nia said.

Assuming there are any lecturers left alive.

Nia felt her stomach grow cold. *Gobaith's right. Who*

knows what we'll see when we finally get to Atlantis. I'd better prepare myself for that. Her buoyant mood hardened into a grim resolve. "Let's go."

Nia and Corwin followed Gobaith through a main archway in the outermost circle of stones. Gobaith turned to the left and went along the curving corridor between the two stone rings until they came to another main archway leading inward. This archway had doors of bronze, but they were greenish, rusted. Luckily they were open.

"It looks like no one's been here for a long time," Nia said.

"Let's hope everything still works," Corwin said.

We must trust that it does, Gobaith sent, *or else our journey ends here.*

Beyond was another doorway, set into an archway of blue stone. This double door was made of gold, and closed. A carving of the sun with ten rays was embossed across both panels. The sun had huge eyes, like a Farworlder. There were no handles on the door.

Corwin went up to it and shoved on one of the door panels. It didn't budge. "Is there a lock I don't see? Or will we have to find some other way in?"

This place was built by my kind, for Farworlders to use, Gobaith sent. *I will have to unlock it.* Gobaith flattened himself against the door, placing each of his tentacles into the grooves that were the sun's rays. He had to stretch to fit, since he wasn't a fully grown Farworlder yet. There came a sudden, flickering glow around Gobaith's body. And the door clicked.

Push it open, please, Gobaith sent.

Nia and Corwin pushed on the right panel of the golden door, and slowly it opened inward. Gobaith stayed stuck against the door until it was half open. Then he swam quickly into the enclosure, over Nia's and Corwin's heads. As soon as they let go of the door panel, it snapped shut again with a boom. Gobaith could have lost a limb if he hadn't been fast enough.

Ahead of them stood the glowing purple crystal, taller than Corwin. At the foot of the towering gem was a platform covered with strange symbols. Gobaith beckoned to them with the tip of a tentacle. *Come. Hurry.*

Nia and Corwin swam up beside Gobaith and stood on the platform. Gobaith went between them, wrapping half of his tentacles around Nia's waist, the other half around Corwin's. *Forgive me—I will need some of your energy.*

Nia felt herself being drained and saw Corwin slumping to her right. But there was little time to worry. The crystal began to glow brighter and brighter until she couldn't look directly at it. Then the world turned inside out.

Chapter Four

Corwin felt like he'd been punched in the stomach. Energy was drained from his very core and he fell against Gobaith and Nia. He hoped his falling wouldn't ruin the spell, but he couldn't do anything about it—his limbs were weak and semiparalyzed. He couldn't move. He was beginning to hate that sensation. It was happening way too often.

It's for your own protection, Gobaith told him. *You must not move as we travel through the unis.*

Corwin dared open his eyes, hoping that didn't count as "moving." Then he wished he hadn't. Nothing he saw made sense. The ringed structure, the crystal, the sea, none of it was there anymore. Lines radiated out from a central point ahead of them, as if they were going down an impossibly long tunnel. Images flickered around them: people in strange clothing, carrying strange objects. He saw snow-covered craggy peaks and impossibly bleak deserts, vast expanses of ice and seas of sand. He saw buildings of such regular shape and amazing height that they couldn't have been built by humankind, and vehicles traveling faster than any chariot or carriage. Corwin didn't know if he was floating in air or water. It seemed to be neither. He wondered how he could breathe. Then he realized he wasn't breathing.

His stomach lurched as Gobaith turned and flew through the wall of the tunnel, entering a narrow tunnel that spiraled around them like the inside of a whelk shell. Corwin's direction sense was completely gone. He didn't know up from down or left from right, let alone north from south. He concentrated on not throwing up on Gobaith. Sneaking a glance at Nia, he saw that she was curled up against Gobaith, her eyes tightly shut. Corwin decided that was a good idea and shut his eyes firmly, too.

He couldn't tell how much time was passing. The very question seemed foolish.

Suddenly, he was cold. Extremely cold. As if his body had turned to ice all at once. He opened his mouth to scream, but he couldn't. He had no breath. *This must be death,* he thought. *Ma'el somehow found us and delivered a final blow.*

Corwin was being pressed in upon from all sides, as if he

were being crushed in the fist of a giant. *Is this the kraken, squeezing the life out of me? I wish I could open my eyes— no, I'm glad I can't. I don't want to see. Good-bye, Nia. . . .*

"Oh, Corwin!" He heard her voice by his ear. "I'm so sorry! I didn't prepare you for this."

Prepare? How does one prepare for death?

Warm hands touched his shoulders. They became even warmer, until they were hot, almost burning. But the warmth spread across his back, down into his legs, up into his head and around into his chest and arms. The pressure began to ease and his gills flapped open, sucking in water and air from the water surrounding him. He was still in the sea, but the water was very cold and strangely thick. It was difficult for his gills to draw oxygen out of it.

At last Corwin could move again, and he opened his eyes. But it was absolute darkness. He couldn't see any-thing, except for a vague greenish glow in the distance.

"Am I blind now?" he managed to burble in the thick water.

"No, no. Your eyes will have to adjust, too."

"Where *are* we? Did something go wrong?"

"We're in the Great Deep, Corwin. I should have warned you. It's not like the sea in the shallows near your land. Down here, there's so much water overhead pressing down that the sea is compressed, and it takes great strength to withstand it. And there's no sunlight down here, so it's very dark and very cold. Hold still while I help your eyes adjust."

Corwin felt her very warm palms cover his eyelids. "Is this going to—"

"Yes."

"Ow!" For a moment it felt as though red-hot pennies had been placed on his eyes—but only for a moment. The pain faded as Nia took away her hands.

Corwin blinked his eyes open. And gasped. There before him was the grandest sight he'd ever beheld. A crystal dome, higher than any mountain he'd seen or heard of, rose high into the sea. Blue-green lights blazed from within it, shining like the brightest stars. Delicate towers rose beneath the crystal dome, glimmering and shimmering in the light as if they'd been carved from pearls and opals. It was more wondrous than the fairy-land of legends. And he could tell, from what he knew of the towers' height from Nia's memories, that the dome was still a couple of miles away.

"That's Atlantis?"

"Yes."

"It's . . . it's so . . . big!"

"Yes." Nia sighed.

Surprised to hear sorrow in her voice, Corwin turned. Her slack, blank face was a picture of devastation. "Nia, what's wrong? You're home. We made it! We're here, at the most wonderful city in the world!"

"You don't see it," Nia said softly. "You can't. You haven't been here before. But it's not what it was."

Corwin frowned, baffled. He couldn't imagine how Atlantis could have been more beautiful. He gently put his arms around Nia. "It may not be what it was, but that's why you've come back, isn't it? So that we can make it all right again? Your people need you to be strong, Nia, so that we can finish this. So that you can be truly home."

"You're right," Nia said, but her body was stiff and her hands were clenched. She was clearly fighting hard to keep from crying. "You're right."

"Of course I am. Even Gobaith will agree. Um . . . where is Gobaith? Gobaith!"

It took Corwin's newly adjusted sight a moment to spot Gobaith floating, drifting motionless in the water nearby. "Gobaith!" Corwin swam over to the Farworlder and gently grasped and shook him. "Gobaith!"

Please, let me rest. I am spent from the journey.

"But . . . but . . . what are we going to do? We need you!"

Nia came over and took Gobaith in her arms. "The transfer point spell took a lot of his energy. He's going to have to rest."

"But what if Ma'el attacks again?"

"Then we'll have to take care of it ourselves." A cold resolve gleamed in Nia's light eyes, and Corwin knew there was no point in arguing.

"Gobaith? How long do you need to rest?"

Don't know. Ask me again later.

"We'd better hurry up and get to Atlantis before Ma'el knows we're here," Nia said. "If he doesn't already." Nia carried Gobaith at her hip and swam ahead.

Corwin swam after her, trying to adjust to her darker mood, and also trying to get used to swimming in the denser water. It really was a different world down here, different even from the sea above. *There's so much I don't know,* he thought again. *The people . . . the mermyds who built those towers ahead have the knowledge of all the wise, ancient kingdoms that have ever been. Maybe even Hamurabia, if it ever existed and wasn't just a joke of Fenwyck's.*

A fish with huge jaws and long, needlelike teeth swam

by, blue-green lights shining along its side like a string of glowing pearls. It was followed by another fish that had a little light like a lantern hanging from a stick that jutted out from its upper jaw. A jellyfish went pulsing by with lights on its stingers and a mantle that glimmered like sunlight on silk. "Nia, are these fish magical?" he asked in awe.

"I don't think it's magic. It's just the way they are. The same stuff that makes their lights also creates the light for the city. It's harvested and put into globes to hang on street posts and buildings."

As they got closer, Corwin could see that there was a pattern in the way the towers were arranged in the city ahead of them. The city itself had a shape like a circular pyramid, layer upon layer, rising up in the middle. At the very center was a pale tower, topped by a golden spire. "You were so right, Nia. It's beautiful."

Nia sighed. "There should be more light."

Corwin swam to her side and took her hand. Even joined to her thoughts as he so often had been, he couldn't imagine the depth of what she'd lost.

Maybe it's better that the city's so dim and dark, Nia told herself. *Now I won't have to see all the damage*

Ma'el's done. In fact, she kept her gaze fixed on the ocean floor as much as she could. She knew she would have to see it eventually—to face up to the horror she'd caused in her beloved city. But not just yet. She shifted Gobaith on her hip to make the Farworlder more comfortable and gripped Corwin's hand tightly, more grateful than ever that he was here. She didn't think she could bear what she was going to have to see without him.

"Is there a main portal?" Corwin asked, still staring in awe. "If so, is it locked or guarded?"

Nia shook her head. "There's no doorway in and out. Very few mermyds ever leave Atlantis, and we don't exactly welcome visitors."

"But you left, so you have to know some way to get in and out of the dome."

Nia's guilt grew stronger. The closer she moved to Atlantis, the more intense it became—and it seemed as though the reminders of her mistake would be increasing too. "There are always secret ways," she said quietly. "Remember the viaduct we used to get into Castle Carmarthen?"

"It won't be that easy this time, will it?" Corwin asked. "I'm guessing they don't really need an underground water supply here."

"No, but the water within the dome does have to be replenished. The old, dirty water is flushed out and fresh is brought in from the ocean. That's what the filtration tubes do."

"Oh," Corwin said. "And that's where the—"

"Shhh!" *We can't talk about the sword here.*

"Oh. Right. Um, what does Atlantis need a dome for anyway," Corwin asked, changing the subject, "if there's water inside and out?"

"It lessens the pressure from the water above it. Once we're inside, we won't need our powers to keep from being crushed."

"That's a relief," Corwin said. "I'm starting to understand how a lump of silver in a coin press feels. Wait, why am I tasting ashes on the water? Is something burning? Nothing can burn down here, can it?"

"No, not usually." Nia also tasted the faint, minerally tang of ash, and it was just as she'd feared—the memories rushed back. Memories of swimming in the worker tunnels . . . with Cephan. She pictured the handsome, dark-haired mermyd as he'd been then, when he'd seemed kind and gentle and sweet. When she'd thought she would be happy to spend the rest of her life with him. She remembered his brash smile and strong arms—and the anger and guilt began to boil inside of her. *How could he have used me like that? How could I have been so stupid as not to see what he really was? How could I have let him trick me into opening the door for Ma'el?*

"What are you thinking about?" Corwin asked. "I can sense the emotions flowing off you, but they're spinning like the whirlpool—"

"I don't want to talk about it," she cut him off.

"Oh." Corwin's mouth turned down at the corners, and his eyes filled with hurt.

"There are things you don't want me to see in *your* thoughts and feelings, aren't there?" Nia asked.

There was a hopeful lift to Corwin's eyebrows. "I guess so."

"Why don't we just focus on what we have to do next?"

"But I—well, okay," Corwin agreed.

Nia could feel his curiosity, in his gaze and his thoughts. But she couldn't let herself dwell on all the sadness she felt. "The ashes we're tasting," she said in a crisp tone, "come from the fumaroles beneath the city. There's an enormous crack in the Earth, through which very hot water rises. Atlantis uses this water to heat the city and power its currents." Nia realized she sounded like one of the instructors at the Academy, and she almost laughed at herself.

"So will we be warmer, once we get inside?" Corwin asked.

"Yes," Nia said with a sigh. "If Ma'el has kept the works running."

"Why wouldn't he?"

"Why would he bother? He and Joab have the power to keep themselves warm and comfortable. Why run the machinery to do it? It would just be another nuisance to him."

"So if the works are running," Corwin began, "that means there are other Atlanteans alive, Atlanteans Ma'el wants to *keep* alive."

Nia turned and gazed at Corwin. "You're right," she said slowly. "It would mean that."

"Then maybe we should look for clues that the works are running." Corwin swam right up to the crystal dome and peered inside.

Pulling Gobaith alongside of her, Nia swam up beside Corwin. She was afraid to look. She was afraid to see a dead city and know that it was all because of what she'd done.

Bubbles flowed swiftly past them, inside the dome. "The rim current's flowing!" Nia cried. "That means the works are operating, at least a little. That means at least some of my people are still alive!" She smiled at Corwin and hugged Gobaith, hope surging up inside her. Peering closer, Nia thought she saw a mermyd, wearing a white tunic, swimming past a nearby building, but the mermyd was gone from sight too soon.

"Maybe we shouldn't stay here," Corwin suggested. "If one of Ma'el's minions sees us, we could be in serious trouble."

"Yes. You're right again," Nia said, although it was hard to pull herself away from the view. With the bubbles forming a veil, she couldn't clearly see whether there had been damage to the buildings. She could almost imagine that the city was still the same as it had been before Garun's Naming ceremony and that she could just go home to the Bluefin Palace and forget everything that had happened. She felt Corwin's hand on her shoulder.

"Nia, we really should leave. Which way do we go again?"

"Oh. Sorry. Of course. Um, I think it's this way." Actually, Nia wasn't sure. But the city was circular, and eventually they would have to come to the filtration tubes no matter which way they went. She shifted Gobaith back to her hip. "Are you all right, Gobaith?"

He blinked his enormous golden eyes sleepily at her.

Getting better. The rest is helping. Wake me if you need me. His eyes closed again.

As they swam alongside the dome, Corwin kept stealing glances at the city. "How can they build towers that high?"

Nia frowned, confused by the question. "I don't know, they just do. Things aren't as . . . heavy underwater as they are on land. Maybe that's why our buildings are taller. Or maybe Atlantis just knows more about it."

"The wisdom of the ancients," Corwin said, almost reverently. "There must be so much your people know, so much they've seen, over time. I wish I could learn more about the city's history."

Nia saw that hunger in his eyes again. She smiled. "They're your people, too, you know. And we have places in the city, archives, where books and scrolls and other writings are preserved—containing knowledge about everything. After we defeat Ma'el, I'll show them to you."

"I'd like that," Corwin said. Then he frowned. "But your . . . I mean, Atlanteans speak a different language than I do. What am I going to do if I have to talk to someone?"

Nia's eyebrows raised. "The same thing I did when I

came to Wales, I'm sure," she replied. "Because of our—
our bond, you should be able to understand anyone we
speak to, and as I start thinking in Atlantean again, so
will you, and you'll learn my language. It'll probably be
awkward and strange at first, but you'll get used to it."

"Oh." Corwin grinned in embarrassment. "So there
are some advantages to this mental bond thing after all."

"A few," Nia said with a smile.

"But that means we'll be in each other's heads more,
and we'll know each other's thoughts and feelings more,
won't we?"

"Um, yes, I guess so."

"Well, I can't wait for that."

Nia couldn't tell if he was being serious or making a
joke. Or maybe both.

The taste of ashes became stronger, and the water
became a bit warmer. Nia knew they must be headed in
the right direction. "We should be there soon."

"So, what exactly are we looking for?" Corwin asked.
"I mean, I've never seen a filtration tube before."

"It should be a big, round door," Nia said. "Actually I
don't know what it looks like on the outside. But I know
I'll recognize it when I see it."

"And . . . the other thing?"

"If we're lucky," Nia added more softly, "it will be lying in the sand nearby."

"Could you . . . send me a mental image of it? So, you know, I won't mistake some other sea garbage for it. It might save time."

Nia wanted to splash him, but that wasn't possible since they were both already in the water. Still, she could understand why he'd be curious, and she couldn't see why it would be a problem. She put her forehead against his and remembered Eikis Calli Werr as it had hung on Dyonis's wall not so long ago—

A long, tapering, silvery blade, inscribed and embellished with water symbols and its name in flowing Atlantean letters, near the guard at the base of the hilt. The hilt itself was wrapped in sharkskin and held the magical oculus. Nia could tell that Corwin was impressed with the weapon, that he could imagine himself wielding it. *Remember,* Nia thought at him, *it was made to be a sword of peace. We have to be careful how we use it.*

"And if we don't find it?" Corwin asked at last.

Nia sighed as she drew away from him. "We've come all this way. I guess we'd have to do the best we can without it."

Corwin paused thoughtfully, staring at the seabed.

Nia glanced beyond him and saw a large circular hole in the dome ahead. "Corwin—I think that's the tube!" She swam to the opening and looked around. The big, round outer hatch to the tube lay on the sea floor, the hinges bent and broken. Peering inside, Nia saw that the piping along the roof of the tube was also bent. "Yes, I think this is it."

She circled around the fallen hatch, peering at the sand of the sea floor for the sword. In the dark of the deep sea, it was hard to see anything, even with her well-adapted eyes. She hoped there might be a reflection of the lights of Atlantis on the blade, if it had been thrown out of the tube. There was no sign of it. She gently jiggled Gobaith on her hip. "Gobaith. Gobaith, are you awake?"

Hmmm? I am now. What is it?

"We're at the filtration tube."

She felt faint thoughts of fear and horror escape from the Farworlder. Gobaith shuddered a little on her hip, clearly remembering the fight in which Garun was killed, when Gobaith was just an infant. *The bad place. We're there already?*

"It took us a while to get here, but you were asleep. But now we need to look for . . . the you-know-what. Can you feel its presence nearby?"

Gobaith blinked up sleepily at her. After a pause, he sent, *No. I sense you and Corwin but no other oculus out here.*

"I suppose that *would* have been too easy," Nia murmured. She swam back to the tube entrance. Corwin was just swimming into it. "Be careful."

"I've never seen anything like this!" Corwin said. "There's no mortaring—it's as though this tunnel was carved from one stone."

"It's a kind of poured, malleable stone," Nia said, squinting as she tried to remember her Academy lessons. "Anyway, do you see . . . *it* in here?"

"No."

"Gobaith doesn't sense its presence either. If Ma'el found it first . . ." Nia felt a wave of despair wash over her.

Don't lose hope, Gobaith sent. *Ma'el's clearly not using the sword. We couldn't have defeated his traps if he were.*

"Then where is it?"

It might have been carried farther out to sea. Or someone else has found it and doesn't know its power. Or Ma'el might have it in his possession but just isn't using it.

"That's almost as bad, isn't it?" Nia asked.

You can't give up hope, Gobaith urged again. *That's what Ma'el wants. We've only just begun to look for the sword.*

Nia swallowed hard. "You're right, Gobaith. As long as I'm alive, I'll keep trying." She swam down the tube to Corwin, who had his hands on the long metal bar in the middle of the inner hatch. "How does this work?" he asked.

Nia tried to remember what Cephan had done. "I think you have to turn it—the bar."

No. He won't be able to open it.

Corwin turned and looked at Gobaith. "Why not?"

The pressure from the outside water will hold it closed.

"Can we do a spell to hold back the pressure, like the spell that keeps the pressure off of us?" Corwin asked.

We can only do one spell at a time, Gobaith sent. *If we hold back the pressure in the tube, then we won't need the spells on our bodies. But I don't have very much strength right now. We will have to get through the door quickly before the spell fades and we're crushed.*

"It's worth the risk, isn't it?" Nia asked.

Corwin sighed, bubbles streaming from his mouth. "If I can't open the door in time, being crushed against it doesn't sound like a worthy end to our mission."

Nia considered the situation. "Gobaith, if we can make the pressure in our part of the tunnel just a little less than it is inside the dome, won't that help Corwin open the door?"

Possibly. If the door latch itself isn't stuck. But if I gauge the spell wrong and the pressure is too low, the water from inside may push us outside the spell, causing us to be crushed anyway.

"Just a little while ago, you were the one telling us not to give up hope, Gobaith!"

Just letting you know the risk.

Nia turned to Corwin. "Can you accept that risk?"

"Do we have any better choices?"

Nia paused. "I don't know of any other way in."

"And it might take us hours to find one. During which time, Ma'el could find us. I say we'd better take the risk."

Nia nodded. "Have I told you lately how brave you are, Corwin?"

"No," Corwin replied with a grin, "but I'd appreciate it if you'd tell me more often. I might just start to believe it."

Nia grinned back. "I'll try to remember that."

Corwin wrapped both his hands around the bar of the tunnel hatch. "Is there anything I can do?" Nia asked Gobaith.

Just hold me up. This will all have to happen very quickly. Be prepared to move fast.

"We will."

Corwin, be sure to swim back from the hatch as soon as it's unlocked.

Corwin nodded once to show that he understood and was ready. Nia held up Gobaith, his tentacles pointed toward the outer opening of the tube. He stretched out all ten of his tentacles until they radiated outward from his body in a circle. Nia could feel Gobaith pulling strength from her body, and she didn't fight it.

Suddenly a pulse of energy flowed from Gobaith's tentacles. An energy wall—precisely the circumference of the tube—moved down along the tunnel, pushing back some of the water. Nia felt a weight come off of her that she'd barely been aware of. Gobaith held the wall about halfway down the tube. *Now! Hurry!*

Corwin grunted as he spun the bar. There came a loud click. "I think I got—"

The hatch slammed open, shoving Corwin into the side of the tube.

"Corwin!" Nia cried.

"I'm all right!" he answered. He pushed himself away from the side of the tube, rubbing the back of his head. Luckily, the hatch hadn't pinned him against the wall.

I can't hold this much longer!

"Nia, swim through!"

"No, you first. I've got to hold Gobaith!"

No, he's right, Nia. We have to go out first and then he must close the hatch right behind us.

There wasn't time for questioning, so Nia swam out through the hatch opening, Gobaith still under her arm. The circular energy wall traveled forward with them. As they passed through the opening, Gobaith sent, *Now, Corwin, start closing the hatch!*

Corwin tugged at the inner latch. "It won't close! The pressure's holding it open!"

That will change as soon as I let go of the spell! Try to close the hatch just a little.

Corwin tugged and tugged and kicked and kicked. Nia decided she had to do something. She extended her arm toward the hatch and used her summoning energy to pull on the hatch door. It was just enough to get the hatch angled back toward them—

I'M BREAKING THE SPELL!

"Corwin!"

He let go of the door and arrowed through the tube opening just as the wall of denser water hit the hatch. It slammed shut again with a loud, echoing *boom*. Again Corwin was thrown across the passageway into the opposite wall. Nia thought she saw the hatch bulge outward for just a moment before it settled into place. Gobaith went limp in her arms.

"Gobaith, are you okay?"

But the Farworlder was asleep again.

"Someone might ask if Corwin was okay, but I guess *he's* not very important."

"Oh, I'm sorry, Corwin. Are you——?"

"Yes, yes, I think so." He rubbed his head and a tiny cloud of blood drifted into the water.

"I think you're hurt." Nia swam over to him and raised her unoccupied hand to the side of his head.

"Just a scratch," Corwin grumbled. "But my head feels like a gourd that's been used for a kick-ball."

"Oh, Corwin, I'm so sorry." Nia let go of Gobaith, letting the Farworlder drift, and she put both hands to Corwin's head. She used a little bit more of her strength to take away his pain.

"Mmmm, that's better," Corwin said. "But I think if we wanted to enter secretly, we've ruined that chance. We must have announced to the whole city that we're here."

"Atlantis is a big city," Nia said soothingly. "There are loud noises all the time. And if anyone decides to investigate, it'll take them a while to get here. This area was deserted even before Ma'el." Nia focused her energy on her fingertips and worked on sealing shut the cut on Corwin's head. This put their faces very close together.

Nia could feel the warmth radiating across his cheeks. Corwin's eyes were such an interesting, mysterious gray. His lips were quite shapely. Nia wondered what it would feel like if she just moved a little closer and—

Voices could be heard on the water. Mermyds were headed their way.

Chapter Five

Corwin cursed his luck. He'd been thinking about kissing Nia and had thought she might not mind. Now he was scanning the corridor, looking for a place to hide.

"This way!" Nia said, tugging on his arm.

"But—"

"Shhh!"

Corwin let Nia lead him, assuming she knew the area better than he did. But weren't they swimming right into the mermyds they needed to hide from?

Nia scooped up Gobaith and swam down the passageway so quickly that it was hard for Corwin to keep up. The passageway was like the filtration tube, smooth stone without joints or mortar. But moss was growing on the walls, and there were objects—tools, maybe—and bits of woven baskets littering the floor.

Nia took a hard left turn and swam up an angling passageway. They came out at what looked like a marketplace.

There were booths and stalls covered with thick, ropy fishnet that seemed to have been built from the planks of sunken ships. A broad tiller had become the top of a display table, and broken masts had become tent poles, with tattered sails used as tent cloth. Piles of baskets were heaped here and there, and Corwin wondered whether they belonged to the mermyd fishmonger women who would sing for customers to buy their catch. But the market was deserted and looked like it had been for a while.

"Here! Let's hide here," Nia whispered, pointing to the highest pile of broken baskets. Nia stuffed Gobaith into one of the larger, handled baskets and then slipped between the pile and the wall. Corwin followed Nia and crouched down beside her.

As they waited and waited, Corwin was tempted to ask what had happened to the people they were avoiding. But a glance at Nia's grim face told him to keep silent, keep waiting.

Suddenly a group of six mermyds swam into the marketplace: two women, four men. They were all wearing white tunics trimmed with black. They looked frightened but determined. The mermyds glanced around the marketplace and began to speak to one another. Corwin concentrated on trying to understand, through Nia's mind, what they were saying.

"Tigala na fipos ya—Are you certain the noise came from here?" said one mermyd.

Corwin listened, fascinated, as his ears heard strange words but his mind knew the meaning of them.

"It was definitely this direction," another said. "Something very large must have fallen to make such a noise."

"Well, nothing's fallen here. We'd better go look in the access tunnels."

"Do we have to? We don't know what could be lurking down there."

"Stop whining and come on. We'll get in trouble if we aren't thorough."

The mermyds swam right past the stack of baskets and down the passageway Nia and Corwin had used just moments before.

"Maybe a sinking ship struck the dome," one was saying in the distance.

"Or there's a volcano erupting in the rift below."

"Maybe those land-dweller wizards we were warned about have attacked at last."

"Ssh! You've been listening to rumors too much."

Corwin turned to Nia. "Is this—"

She clamped her hand over his mouth and put her forehead against his again. *Sound carries a long distance in water*, she reminded him. *Wait before you speak.*

Corwin waited, impatiently. He peered through the baskets at the marketplace. There was a strong fishy taste in the water, as well as the taste of rotting wood and rope. He almost expected the ghosts of drowned sailors and fishermen to drift in and out of the booths.

Finally Nia spoke again, softly. "They should be far enough away now. I wonder why they were all wearing white."

"Is that important?" Corwin asked.

"Yes—but I don't know what it means. White's the color of death, to my people. No clan ever wore clothing of just that color. Did you see how thin they were? They can't be eating well. And that group was mixed-clan. Two were from the Starfish clan, and another was from the Orcas."

"So, what does all this *mean*?" Corwin asked.

Nia's face was pale in the dim light. "Ma'el has completely overturned the social order. Nothing is the same."

"Did you expect everything to be the same?" Corwin asked, a bit baffled.

"I don't know. When I saw that some of my people were still alive I . . . I had hoped . . ."

Corwin got the strong impression that Nia was about to cry. He put his arm around her, but she gently pushed it aside.

"No. We have a saying that the sea doesn't need more saltwater. I don't have time to cry."

Corwin settled for patting her shoulder.

Suddenly, someone else swam into view. Or, actually, some*thing*. It was a dolphin, with a box strapped to its back. It paused in the center of the marketplace and bobbed its head as if sniffing around.

"Ki-ki!" Nia blurted out, and to Corwin's shock, she rushed out from behind the pile of baskets.

When the dolphin saw her, Corwin could swear the creature's grin got wider and happier. It did a swim-dance around Nia, like a dog overjoyed to see its master. Nia squeaked at it and rubbed its head and kissed its nose.

"Nia, shouldn't we be hiding?" Corwin asked. "What if those other mermyds come back?"

"You don't understand, Corwin," Nia replied, her voice filled with joy for the first time he could remember. "This is Ki-ki. She served my family for years. I'm so glad she's all right."

"Yes, well, that's all well and good, but let's hope Ki-ki doesn't get us kill-killed."

Nia opened the box on the dolphin's back and pulled out a white tunic. Then she pulled out another one. "Look! Disguises!" She tugged one of the tunics over her head and put it on. It was a little big and baggy on her. She handed the other to Corwin.

Corwin grudgingly tugged it on. It was a tight fit and didn't hang much below his waist. He was glad to be wearing breeches. "Maybe we should swap."

But the voices were coming back.

"I told you we wouldn't find anything."

"There was the damage to that filtration tube door."

"It's stress from the water pressure, I'm telling you. Someone should have fixed the outer hatch weeks ago. The inner hatch wasn't made to hold back The Deep this long."

"Our new Avatar and King have other things occupying their minds."

"They won't have minds left to occupy if that door blows."

"No time to change clothes," Nia whispered. She took up the basket that held Gobaith and said something to Ki-ki. Then she motioned to Corwin to take hold of one of Ki-ki's side fins. As he did so, she slapped Ki-ki's tail and the dolphin shot straight up with a thrashing of its powerful tail. They entered a vertical tube that was much smaller and narrower than the filtration tunnel—there was barely room for the three of them and the basket holding Gobaith.

Corwin heard the white-clad mermyds enter the marketplace below them, and he dared a glance down. None of the group bothered to look up. *It's just like Fenwyck used to say: People won't bother to look for what they don't expect to see.*

Higher and higher Ki-ki carried them up the tube, until it ended, letting them out in a huge, dark room with walls of gray stone. Not much of the light from the city outside penetrated in through the wide windows. The room was filled with long tables, also made of stone, but no chairs or other furnishings. Clay jugs and urns were stacked in the corners, and baskets like the one Gobaith was in littered the floor.

"Is this some sort of *factorium*?" Corwin asked, using the awkward Latin word because there was no good word in his language that explained such a place.

"Food is . . . was prepared here for the noble families," Nia replied. "I guess it's not needed now, but it's still sad to see it deserted like this."

Ki-ki swam slowly around the room, nosing into some of the baskets. Nia went to one of the broad, shutterless windows. Corwin joined her there and gazed out at the city of Atlantis.

Spires and towers and balustrades and porticos and buttresses shimmered and glimmered in the blue-green light. Some buildings were faced with mother-of-pearl, some faced with colorful tiles of sand and coral. The highest tower at the center of the city was built of white marble that seemed to glow, and its spire was made of gold. Here and there, mermyds in white would flit between the buildings, some carrying little spheres emitting blue-green light. *It's so beautiful,* Corwin thought. He could have stared at it for hours. *Except,* he reminded himself, *we don't have hours to spare.*

"It's so dismal," Nia sighed beside him.

Corwin blinked. "If this is dismal, it must have been an amazing sight before," he marveled.

"It was. And I never appreciated it. There used to be mermyds swimming everywhere. They'd all be wearing clothes whose colors showed what family they were from, or suits of sea-dragon-scale armor if they were palace guards. And there'd be dolphins and sea turtles carrying messages or giving people rides. That plaza over there used to be filled with merchants' booths selling all sorts of wonderful things—pearls and coral and treasures from sunken ships. That building over there was the Academy where we all went to school. And you can't see it from here, but that way is the Great Arena where they held races and . . ."

". . . and the trials for Avatar," Corwin finished for her.

"Yes." Nia let out a deep sigh. "I have to stop doing this. I have to forget about what was, what I've lost, and just concentrate on the next step."

"Right," Corwin said. He paused. "Um, so what *is* the next step?"

"I have to go to the Bluefin Palace, and see if I can learn what's happened to my family."

"Nia!" Corwin wanted to shake her. "Are you sure that's the best idea? I mean, isn't that the first place Ma'el would be expecting you to go? If he's going to set traps for us, that would be the likely place, don't you think?"

Nia turned and glared at him. "We need allies, Corwin. We're not going to be able to attack Ma'el in his lair by ourselves. He'll be too strong for us. Family members are the strongest allies you can have. You may be right, it is a risk. But we need a place to hide and plan. We need to learn what's happened here and whether anyone will fight with us. And we'll need help finding the you-know-what. Maybe my mother or . . . Pontus will have left a clue. We have to start somewhere."

Corwin could feel how desperately Nia wanted to go home, to see something familiar again. *Maybe she's right. I don't know this city or these people. Maybe our best chance is to go to her home to look for survivors. Maybe there won't be a trap.*

But I wouldn't bet on it.

"Well, okay then," he said. "I guess I just have to trust you. But promise me that we'll leave at the first sign of any ambush. I don't think poor Gobaith is up to pulling our chestnuts out of the fire again just yet."

Nia nodded. "I understand. We'll be careful. Ki-ki!"

The dolphin came swimming eagerly over.

"Are you sure it's a good idea," Corwin began, "to bring the animal with us— Ooof!" The dolphin had given him a playful nudge in the stomach that sent him drifting into the wall.

Nia sighed. "As you can see, she'd be good in a fight. Wouldn't you, Ki-ki?" Nia bobbed her head at the dolphin.

Ki-ki nodded back and opened her mouth to display lots of sharp teeth.

"Aha," Corwin said, not certain he felt relieved as he

circled warily around the dolphin. "Does she understand what you're saying?"

"She knows some Atlantean commands and a lot of gestures. Some mermyds say dolphins are almost as smart as we are. Land-dwellers have creatures you train in the same way, right?"

"Yes. Dogs," Corwin said. "Only most dogs aren't that big and powerful, and they don't have quite as many teeth."

Nia smiled. "Come on, let's go."

Ki-ki squeaked and Corwin hefted Gobaith's basket onto Ki-Ki's back. Nia took one fin and Corwin took the other, and out the window they went.

It was amazing to Corwin, to swim *over* the beautiful city, the streets and lights mostly below them. It was like flying, but slowly, and with no fear of falling. *This must be how birds see the world,* he thought. *But better. I'll bet even Nag would envy me.* It was wonderful, enchanting, like a dream.

It's horrible, frightening, like a nightmare, Nia thought as she gazed at the darkened, empty city below. Familiar landmarks were still there, but the mermyd citizens that had once made the places come alive were gone.

Memories assaulted her—there was the place where she'd bought her first gown with her own money earned as a palace guard. Over there was where Nia had heard a Bluefin elder tell her she was qualified to be considered for the Trials for Avatar. And over *there* was where she and Cephan had sneaked on their first "date."

But now there was no laughter of children and dolphins, no mermyds racing each other through the corridors between buildings, no palaces gaily lit with parties. Just a few remaining mermyds flitting about like ghosts on unknown errands for an evil king. *Or maybe I'm misjudging them and they've escaped or rebelled against Ma'el,* Nia thought. *But how can I ask one without risking being betrayed to Ma'el? If only I could find one relative hiding in my family's palace, or even just one friend who could reassure me and tell me everything's going to be all right.*

Ki-Ki unerringly guided them back to the Bluefin Palace. Nia paused and stared up at the coral stone tower with its mother-of-pearl facing, and had to fight back tears again.

"This is where you grew up?" Corwin asked.

"Yes," Nia said. "My family's lived here for generations."

"It's . . . impressive. King Vortigern himself would drop dead with envy."

"Thanks. It's not the grandest place in Atlantis. But it's home." Nia didn't quite understand the baffled look Corwin was giving her. After all, nearly every family of any consequence in Atlantis lived in a palace. Nia gazed back at the tower and was shocked to see that the Bluefin emblem, which had hung on the tower wall, had been removed. Nia clenched her fists. *Who would insult my family like that?* The answer was obvious. *Only Ma'el would be so cruel.*

"If Vortigern had known you came from this," Corwin went on, "he'd have allied with you in a heartbeat. In fact, he probably would have insisted you marry his son."

This jolted a laugh out of Nia. "That young monster, Vortimer? Never! I'd marry Ma'el first—" Nia covered her mouth and looked around, but no one was nearby that she could see. "No, I wouldn't, actually. But, really, this place isn't as special as you think. Most people live in palaces in Atlantis. It's different from your world."

"That's sure the truth," Corwin said, his eyes wide.

Ki-ki squeaked and nudged Nia gently to get her attention. "What is it, Ki-ki?"

The dolphin swam around the corner of the building and tossed her head to indicate that Nia should follow. "Come on, Corwin. Ki-ki's found something."

"The last time I had a pet find something," Corwin grumbled, "it was the start of this whole mess."

Nia followed the dolphin down and down to a lower floor of the Bluefin tower. There was a light moving around in the lowermost hall, a formal room for receiving guests. Nia hadn't gone into this room very often—her sleeping chamber was higher up the tower, along with the informal family dining chamber.

Nia peered in through the window. Glow lamps were hanging in the corners of the chamber. There was a niche in the far end where another symbol of the Bluefin clan had been hung. The niche was empty now. Someone moved out of the shadows up to the niche—a female fish-tailed mermyd in a golden dress. She placed something in the niche and then swam back. Once the mermyd moved away, Nia could make out what she'd hung up—it was the symbol of the Sunfish clan, here in the Bluefin Palace! Nia sucked in her breath, shocked. Why would anyone do that?

Then the mermyd swam into the light, and Nia's heart nearly stopped with joy. "Callimar!" Nia went in through the open window, not bothering to fight back the tears.

Callimar's mouth dropped open. "Nia!"

"What are you *doing* here?" they both burst out at once.

Nia rushed up to her best friend and hugged her fiercely. Callimar tentatively hugged back.

Nia let go and gazed at Callimar, amazed at how much she'd changed in so little time. Callimar was still a classic mermyd beauty, with dark, emerald green hair, golden eyes, fin-shaped ears. But she had aged and already didn't seem anything like the carefree youth she'd been so recently. Nia realized with a start that the same could probably be said about her, though she couldn't remember the last time she'd looked at her reflection that closely.

"Nia, you look terrible, poor thing!" Callimar said, confirming Nia's worry. "Where have you been hiding all this time?"

"Um, around," Nia said, not wanting to reveal too much too soon. "But I'm so glad to see you alive and well. How have you managed with the . . . changes here? You're not even wearing white like everyone else."

"Oh, um, it's a long story." Callimar's smile had a twist of fear in it, and her gaze kept darting to the windows.

She's afraid that someone could be listening, Nia thought. *We have to be so careful now. So much depends on everything we do and say.* "Yes. We both have long stories." Nia bit her lip, looking over at the Sunfish sign. "But, if you don't mind, could you tell me why you're putting the Sunfish emblem up here, in the Bluefin Palace?"

Callimar's hands fluttered in the water and her eyes widened. "Well, you know, your family isn't here . . . right now, and we were such good friends . . . I just . . . wanted to preserve this place, for, you know, the time when things would be better. When you and your family could come back. I wanted to see that it was taken good care of."

Something didn't quite ring true in Callimar's words. *She's afraid . . . afraid of me! But why?* Softly, gently, Nia asked, "Callimar, what's happened to you? You don't have to be so nervous with me. I've come back to make things right, if I can. To make Atlantis the way it was again. But I need help. I need friends." Nia took Callimar's hand and squeezed it.

Suddenly Callimar glanced behind Nia and jumped back. "Nia—Who's that?"

Nia turned. Corwin had come through the window, Kiki right behind him. "Is everything all right?" he asked.

Nia had to pause a moment to translate Corwin's language, since she'd adjusted so quickly to speaking Atlantean with Callimar. "It's all right, Corwin. This is Callimar. She was my best friend before . . . everything happened." Turning to Callimar, Nia said in Atlantean, "This is Corwin."

"Is he another one of your Stingray clan friends?" Even now, Nia sadly noted, Callimar didn't hide the slight sneer in her voice.

"No," Nia replied. She decided to be cautious, knowing how shocked and even more frightened Callimar might be if she knew that Corwin was part land-dweller. "He's of the . . . Basking Shark clan."

"Nia, there is no Basking Shark clan."

"There is *now*," Nia said firmly, raising her brows.

"Oh," Callimar said. "And why was he talking funny?"

"It's a . . . secret code."

"I see."

"Callimar, we need your help. I'm trusting you because you're my best friend. Corwin and I want to free Atlantis from Ma'el. Don't ask me how, yet, but we might have the power to do it. But we'll need help. Will you help us?"

Callimar's eyes widened even more and she swam back from Nia. "Free Atlantis from Ma'el? Have you gone crazy? Do you know what you're saying? He has all the power of all the kings, and he'll . . ." She covered her mouth with her hand a moment and again glanced around the room. "Nia, there's nothing you and your . . . Basking Shark friend can do. Everything's different now. You just have to accept that."

"I *can't* accept that," Nia said. "I don't understand how you can."

"It's just . . . being sensible, that's all."

Nia felt her stomach rumble and realized she'd been through a lot since she'd last eaten. "Could you . . . could you at least tell us where we could find some food without alerting too many people that we're here? And where we could hide and rest for a while? Believe me, I won't tell anyone that you helped us, if that's what you're afraid of."

Callimar stared at Nia for what seemed like a long time. Finally she spoke. "No, I can't let you wander off by yourselves. It's too dangerous now. You'd better come with me. I'll make sure that you're fed at the Sunfish Palace. And if I can, I'll give you a place to rest."

Nia allowed herself to smile. "I knew I could count on you," she said, hoping it was true.

Callimar returned a sickly smile. "We should leave now, though, before we're seen. Follow me." Callimar headed for the window.

Corwin swam up beside Nia. "Do you trust her?" he asked softly. "From the way she was looking at us, I'm not sure she's your friend anymore."

"What choice do we have? She's our best hope right

now. At least we might be able to find out how things are here from her, even if she can't do much to help."

"If you say so. What about . . . ?" Corwin held up Gobaith's basket.

"Let's not say anything about that, for now."

Corwin nodded. He turned to the dolphin. "Go on, Ki-ki. Shoo!"

"No, no, let Ki-ki come with us," Nia said. In a slightly harder tone, she added, "We might need her later."

"Oh. Sorry." Corwin awkwardly patted the dolphin on the head.

"Come on!" Callimar called from the window.

Nia and Corwin, bringing Gobaith in the big basket, swam after Callimar through the darkened streets. Since the most noble houses tended to build their palaces closest to the rim, where the water was freshest, the Sunfish Palace was right up against the crystal dome. Unlike the other buildings around it, the Sunfish home was full of light. Music played from one of the upper rooms, and Nia thought she could even hear laughter. It almost brought tears to her eyes. "Here, finally, is one place that's just like Atlantis used to be."

"And doesn't that make you wonder?" Corwin muttered.

"You don't like Callimar, do you?" Nia asked.

"I can't tell if I'd like her, but I don't trust her. Fenwyck used to say that anyone healthy and wealthy under the rule of a tyrant is a friend of the tyrant. And yes, Fenwyck would have loved to be such a friend, but I think he was right anyway."

"We'll soon find out, I guess," Nia said.

Callimar led them up to a window leading into a small, private dining chamber on the fifth floor of the palace tower.

"You may go find air, Ki-ki," Nia said to the dolphin, "but come back as soon as you can."

Ki-ki nodded and sped away.

"Find air?" Corwin asked.

"Atlantean dolphins are specially bred to stay underwater longer, but they still need to breathe air now and then," Nia explained. "There are air tanks, like tiny dry rooms, scattered around the city for their use."

Nia followed Callimar in through the window, and after a moment so did Corwin.

"I'm going to go order dinner for us. Please make yourselves comfortable." Callimar left them alone in the dining chamber, leaving through an ornate door of pieced coral.

"I was wrong," Corwin said. "Vortigern wouldn't just envy this place. He'd *die* of envy."

Nia gazed around, realizing why Corwin was so

impressed. The floor was inlaid marble with geometric patterns of octopuses and fishes. Delicate wall-hangings of pearls, gold and topaz beads undulated against the walls. In the middle of the room was a low malachite table with a net of gold thread draped over it.

"The Sunfish clan was the most wealthy and noble clan in Atlantis," Nia said.

"Looks like they still are."

A nervous servant came in and placed platters of succulent fish rolls and kelp balls under the net so that they wouldn't drift away. The servant tried to take the basket Corwin held, but Corwin scared him off with a grimace and a growl. Another servant brought in bladders of kelp wine and handed one each to Nia and Corwin.

Nia showed Corwin how to suck on the reed straw to drink the kelp wine. He took one sip, made an awful face and put the drink aside. "Ugh! You drink this stuff?"

"I guess it doesn't suit everyone's tastes," Nia said delicately.

"No offense, but I think Anwir's ale was better," Corwin said.

More servants brought in giant clam half-shells, each filled with a cushion, and set these around the table. Callimar came in with them and curled up in one of the shells. She gestured gracefully for Nia and Corwin to do the same.

"Is it safe for us to talk here?" Nia asked as she sat.

"I don't think you could find a safer place," Callimar replied.

Nia took a deep breath. "Then Callimar, can you tell me——" she stopped, her voice shaking. "Can you tell me what happened to my family?" she forced herself to finish.

Callimar sighed and bit into a fish roll. After swallowing, she replied, "I hate to give you sad news." A quake seemed to pass through Nia's body. Her worst fears were true—they were all gone. "Nia," Callimar continued, "the elders of your clan chose to . . . defy the changes in Atlantis. From what I know, they've been put into custody until they come to their senses."

"Wait—then my mother and Pontus might still be alive!" Nia exclaimed, hope filling her again.

Callimar regarded her with obvious sympathy. "Maybe," she said. "I can't say for certain. It would be too dangerous for me to try and find out."

"Of course. I understand. But what about your elders, and other members of the Sunfish clan?"

Callimar paused even longer before replying. "Rather than cause more chaos, my family chose to accept Ma'el's rule and abide by his laws. In exchange for our loyalty, we've been allowed to retain our noble status."

"Aha," Corwin said. He looked at Nia. *Told you so.*

Nia felt her stomach grow cold. "And since the Sunfish are the only noble house left, they gain much more power."

Callimar tossed her head nonchalantly. "Well, yes, I guess that's true."

"Callimar, don't you see how wrong this is?" Nia demanded, leaning toward her friend. "Ma'el is just using you and your family. He's going to destroy everything that Atlantis stood for—peace, equality, knowledge, freedom. All he wants to do is conquer the world!"

Callimar gripped the edge of the table. "And when he's done there will be peace, once and for all. With no barbarian land-dwellers to be afraid of!"

Corwin frowned.

"What do you mean?" Nia asked Callimar. "Why should we be afraid of land-dwellers?"

"Exactly! Atlantis has been living in fear of those air-sucking land-dwellers ever since it sank beneath the surface. Lord Ma'el has said that, in time, once the crisis is past, Atlantis will be able to rise again and we mermyds will be free to roam the world whenever we want."

Nia paused, unable to believe what she was hearing.

"Maybe that's true, but is it worth the cost, Callimar? Ma'el has already bought his rulership here with murder. Now he wants to rule the land-dwelling kingdoms in the same way. How many of them will die before Ma'el's done with his conquest? How many of *us* will die? I don't know how you can think of it as freedom at all if Ma'el has complete power over the world."

Callimar sighed and shook her head. "Nia, why are you trying to swim against the rim current? The fact is that Lord Ma'el has the power. The best thing you can do is save yourself and your family, until times are better.

"We've been told to watch for you, you know," she continued, her tone beginning to grow colder. "Lord Ma'el had great respect for your grandfather, Dyonis. Ma'el wants to form a coalition government with the great houses represented. He even said that he thinks the last Avatarship was stolen from you, and that you have great talents you could offer to the New Atlantis. I'm pretty sure that if you just surrendered yourself to Lord Ma'el, he would release your family and restore your noble house. Don't you think that would be the best thing you could do? If you try to fight him, he'll just destroy you and your family."

Nia's body ached, and she wished she could be anywhere else. Of course Ma'el would burden her with the choice of saving her family over the slim chance of saving Atlantis. *If I fail, how many more will die? But if I don't try, many more will certainly die.* "You don't understand, Callimar. You can't trust any agreements Ma'el makes. He has no loyalty to the Sunfish or anyone else. All he wants is power. He's *evil*, Callimar. How can you serve him?"

Anger and pain warred in Callimar's eyes. Her gills flapped rapidly for a few moments before she replied. "I'm sorry you feel that way, Nia. But I have to be loyal to my family, *my* clan. Ma'el imprisons dissenters in the dry rooms, did you know that? That's probably where your mother and father are. If they are, can you imagine the suffering they've gone through? But the Sunfish clan has stayed strong and loyal. We wouldn't let that happen to each other. None of us would condemn any member of our family to such a fate. We've done what we have to do to *protect* each other."

"To save yourselves while Atlantis falls?" Nia exclaimed, horrified. She'd always known that Callimar was a little self-involved, but this was beyond what she would have expected of someone she'd considered a good friend.

Callimar narrowed her eyes. "Are you calling me selfish? You, who let your cousin be killed by your Deepsider boyfriend Cephan so that *you* could be Avatar?"

The accusation cut through Nia. "That's not true! I tried to stop Cephan!" she cried.

"That's what the gossip says about you, you know," Callimar told her. "They say the last prophecy of the kings was that a traitor would bring down Atlantis. I didn't want to believe it was you, but now I'm beginning to wonder—"

"Stop it, Callimar! You know me better than that! I would never do anything to hurt my family, or Atlantis. If I'd wanted to ruin Atlantis, I'd be standing at Ma'el's side, instead of fighting him. Think, Callimar! Think about what Ma'el's done already. Your clan can't buy off his evil with your loyalty forever. Someday he'll turn against the Sunfish, too, when it suits him. Help me, Callimar— before it's too late."

Callimar closed her eyes and sighed. "I'm so sorry, Nia. I'd hoped you'd do the smart thing. The right thing for your clan. But I've got to look after my own. I can't help you."

Nia sighed too. "I knew I was asking a lot of you. I think Corwin and I had better go now."

Callimar got up from the clamshell chair. "You don't understand, Nia. I can't let you go. My family knows you and your friend are here. If we let you escape, we'll be punished. I can't let that happen. I'll give you one last chance, Nia. Please. Give up this idiotic, suicidal fight."

So that you can turn me in to Ma'el and get extra points for being good minions? Nia thought bitterly. But instead she said, "I'm sorry, Callimar. I can't."

Callimar hung her head and flapped her hand in a beckoning gesture.

"Hey!" Corwin cried out, as four burly Manta Ray guards swam in through the window.

Nia's arms were grabbed by two of them. The other two headed for Corwin. "Callimar!" Nia cried. "Don't let them do this! We may be Atlantis's last hope!"

Callimar looked up sadly. "I'm sorry, Nia. But be brave. You always were good in dry rooms. I hope that . . ." Unable to finish, Callimar covered her face and swam out.

Chapter Six

What's happening? What's happening? Gobaith sent. Corwin was thrilled to hear the young Farworlder's familiar question as the Sunfish household guards grabbed Corwin's arms. "We're being captured!" he yelled.

Let me out! Let me out! The top of the fish basket pounded against Corwin's arm, and Corwin let go of the basket.

Gobaith uncoiled and launched himself at the guards. He flared his tentacles wide in front of them, glaring imperiously and making a screen of bubbles with his siphons.

The action startled the mermyd guards, and they released Corwin and flung their arms up in front of their faces. Corwin swam aside, preparing to fend off another grab. But, strangely, the guards didn't try to seize Corwin again—they simply stared at Gobaith in fear and confusion.

Ki-ki the dolphin zoomed in through the window.

"Ki-ki! Over here! Help!" Nia cried from the other end of the room. The dolphin arrowed in and delivered a blow to the belly to each of Nia's guards with the top of its head and snout.

Corwin and Nia both had the same thought and headed for the window, and escape, at once. "Gobaith!" Corwin cried over his shoulder.

But Nia shook her head. "Let Gobaith delay the guards for a little while longer. We have to get out of here."

Corwin followed her out the window and straight down the outside wall of the Sunfish Palace: then they shot out over the street and into a narrow alley. Nia took a sharp turn around a corner that would hide them from view of the Sunfish Palace. Corwin felt the same surge of exhilaration that he used to feel when he and Fenwyck were fleeing angry fairgoers—the sweet joy of a close escape. But the unfamiliar surroundings and the complication of swimming instead of running caused his pleasure to fade quickly. Nia stopped and slipped beneath an overhanging balcony. "Let's wait under here for Gobaith."

Corwin joined her, relieved at the chance for a brief rest. "Nia, where are we going exactly, other than away?" he asked.

"Callimar said my family's probably being held in a

dry room," Nia replied, her voice firm and decisive. "So I'm going to the one dry room I know of that might be big enough to hold prisoners. Even if my relatives aren't there, we'll have a good chance at finding allies among the mermyds Ma'el has punished."

"Do I get to say I told you so about Callimar?" he couldn't help asking.

Nia's frown deepened. "No. She was my best friend, Corwin. I had to at least try. And like I said, we did learn more about what's going on here from her."

"Yes," Corwin agreed, "but now there's a powerful group of people who know you're back and that we're rebels. I'm not sure it's an even trade. You know, if Fenwyck were here, he'd have suggested we pretend to join the enemy side. That way, we'd be closer to Ma'el and have an easier chance to take a stab at him. Preferably in the back, in the dark, when he least expects it."

Nia shook her head. "I'm starting to get tired of your master Fenwyck, and I've never even met him."

"I can't say I blame you," Corwin muttered. "Some days I wish I never had."

"Besides," Nia went on, "Ma'el isn't stupid. He would never trust us. We've managed to defeat him and his traps so far, so he'll know enough to be careful. We've got to surprise him somehow. That's why I hope he still doesn't know the power of . . . the you-know-what."

"That's assuming *we* can figure out how to use the power of the you-know-what." Corwin wasn't sure how he felt about the prospect of finding a genuine magical sword. Myth and legend weren't very helpful guides in how a person was supposed to use one. Often the myths implied that only one person could wield such a sword—usually you had to be at least a demigod. Despite his new abilities, Corwin didn't feel very godlike. And there was the danger that sometimes these weapons had minds of their own.

An oculus is part of a Farworlder's mind, right? Corwin thought. *But how much of a mind will the sword have? Maybe Gobaith will be able to tell us.* "What *is* keeping Gobaith, anyway?" Corwin asked, glancing back the way they'd come. Corwin tried to contact Gobaith's thoughts, but received only sensations of speed and unalloyed glee.

"Bewildering the Sunfish clan and their guards, no doubt," Nia said. "We're taught from an early age to revere the Farworlders. Very few of us ever get to be in the presence of one. No mermyd would ever raise a hand against a Farworlder. Except for Ma'el, of course. The guards might try to catch Gobaith, but they'd be so careful about it that Gobaith could swim rings around them. Look, here he comes!"

Gobaith zoomed up beside Corwin. *Here I am! Did you miss me?*

"Of course. Did you enjoy yourself?" Corwin asked him.

Not nearly as much as Ki-ki did. But we'd better get to a good hiding place quickly. The Sunfish won't remain confused for long.

Again Nia shook her head. "There's no point in just hiding somewhere, Gobaith. We have to move fast to stay ahead of Ma'el. Let's go. And keep an eye out to make sure we aren't being followed."

Corwin looked around. He didn't see any mermyds following or ahead of them. But who knew who might be lurking within the darkened windows of the towers they swam past? And he couldn't see clearly down in the darkness of the alleyways below.

Corwin had never been in a city this large—its sheer size and strangeness were disturbing despite its beauty. *In Carmarthen, I knew every bolthole, every back door, every street that led quickly out of town and into the forest. Here I know nothing. I must rely on Nia. Or Gobaith, I guess.*

I don't know the city either, Gobaith sent. *I was only a crecheling when I left. I never saw anything but the nursery*

until I was taken out to prepare for the Naming. And after—
wait, there's someone behind us, approaching rapidly!

"Nia!" Corwin cried in what he hoped was a quiet shout.

"This way," she called back, ducking in through the nearest narrow window.

Corwin slipped in too, and Nia immediately grabbed him. She pulled him next to her and they pressed themselves against the wall—which Corwin found harder to do underwater than he'd expected. Gobaith zipped in as well and huddled near their feet.

Outside the building, someone said, "I told you, I saw them come this way."

A heavy sigh. "They could be anywhere by now. We shouldn't have let them get such a head start."

"The Farworlder wouldn't let me get past him."

"We should have captured the Farworlder."

"Do you know what you're saying?"

"We could have been gentle about it! We could have used a net. Now we'll probably be sent to work for Ma'el in the Lower Depths."

"Not if we're careful. You know what Ma'el would have done to the Farworlder."

"That can't be helped, can it? He's in charge now. Now what are we going to do?"

"We can tell them Nia and that boy had help from Farworlder magic. That's how they got away, most likely."

"I hope that works. Come on, let's keep looking a little while longer before we return with our excuses."

The voices began to grow softer, but Corwin made out a few last remarks. "You know, maybe it's a good thing she got away. Maybe she can overthrow Ma'el. She was supposed to be the next Avatar——"

"Are you trying to get us both killed? Somebody could be listening! Watch your tongue."

"Sorry . . ."

The voices faded, and Corwin turned to Nia to see her reaction. She smiled. "Someone's listening, but not who you think," she said softly, gazing toward the window.

Corwin was happy to see Nia smile, but he was anxious to move on. They'd taken shelter in an abandoned home, and as he looked around, he saw a small hammock hung from two posts nearby. A brightly colored toy fish, with one fin broken, floated beside it. This room must have been a child-mermyd's room. A child that might no longer be alive. "Maybe we should get going," he said.

"Not yet," Nia replied. "They're still looking for us, and they might come back."

"One of them sounded like he might be on your side."

"Maybe, but I wouldn't count on his loyalty yet. At least we've learned where Ma'el might be found. That's one thing."

"Yes, as soon as we're ready to face him. But that might be a while."

"Not if we find enough allies quickly," Nia said. "If I can find my family, my . . . mother and—"

"Why do you always pause when you talk about your relatives?" Corwin asked. He'd held the question back before, but the pauses seemed to be getting more pronounced the longer they were in Atlantis.

"It's . . . it's complicated."

"Can't be any worse than my family history," Corwin grumbled.

"My father wasn't really my father," Nia blurted out. "My grandfather was my father. And my mother isn't really my mother. I was adopted by a man who was really my half-brother and raised by a woman who was no blood relation at all."

After a pause, Corwin said, "I take it back. Yours is worse than mine."

"There's more," she said. "I should have told you, I know. I'm sorry. It's just—it's all so much to take in. My mother . . . my *real* mother was a land-dweller."

Corwin's eyebrows shot up. "A land-dweller? Then that means . . ."

Nia nodded, biting her lower lip. "I didn't find out until this whole mess began. Ma'el first told me, but Dyonis, who I had thought was my grandfather, confirmed it. My blood mother died shortly after I was born, and I was given to Pontus and Tyra, who I call my parents. They never told me my true heritage. Atlanteans don't think highly of land-dwellers—"

"I noticed," Corwin growled.

"—so they wanted to spare me the shame. But that was why I could walk in your world for so long without dying. Why I've always been good in dry rooms." Nia fell silent and stared at her feet.

Corwin felt a swell of purely selfish joy. All this time he'd been so worried that there'd never be a real chance for them to be together, because they came from totally different worlds. But now that he knew he was part mermyd and she was part land-dweller . . . "So, you're a halfsie, like me," he teased.

"I guess you could say that. But Atlanteans and land-dwellers are both human, like I told you. Otherwise you and I couldn't exist."

"Of course, but—"

Our pursuers have given up the chase, Gobaith sent. *Corwin's right, we should move on.*

Corwin sighed with annoyance, wondering if the Farworlder had ulterior reasons for interrupting the conversation. Still, with luck, there'd be time to hint at future plans—when they knew they'd *have* a future. "All right. Where do we go from here, Nia?"

"This way."

Corwin followed her out the window and again they swam through the city, faster this time. Corwin was beginning to enjoy the freedom of moving in three dimensions, and he wondered if he would ever be satisfied with just walking again.

Eventually it became clear where Nia was leading them. After a sharp right turn down a broad main thoroughfare, the pale marble of the Farworlder Palace, with its golden spire, glowed before them.

"Nia, are you sure about this?" Corwin said as softly as he could. "What if Ma'el's ruling from this very palace?"

Nia shook her head. "Remember, our pursuers said he was in the Lower Depths. Those are the levels where the fumarole works are, where we first came through. Ma'el wouldn't dare rule from here. It's not a good fortress for someone who wants to hold power by force. It's too open.

There are too many ways in and out. Ma'el would want more control than that."

"Ah," Corwin said, impressed with Nia's reasoning. "You're right. Even Castle Carmarthen had only one main gate, in order to defend against attack."

"Right. So let's hope that Ma'el's headquarters in the Lower Depths has a servant's entrance or two."

As they swam between the outer pillars of the Farworlder Palace, Corwin could see what Nia meant. Broad colonnades of tall, slender columns surrounded the huge building, and many high arches stood before hallways and corridors leading into the interior. The walls were hung with glowing green globes that reflected off of gold- and glass-tiled walls. Plazas with sunken kelp gardens were interspersed between the colonnades. It was an astonishingly beautiful building, and Corwin wondered if this was the way heaven was supposed to look. *Though the angels here would have fins instead of wings*, he thought.

"We just have to make one small detour," Nia said. "As long as we're here."

Should we? I'm afraid, Gobaith sent.

"I have to look," Nia said, "and we might learn something important."

"Look at what?" Corwin asked.

"A . . . place I used to work."

Where I used to live.

"Well, let's go then," Corwin said, feeling like he really didn't have much choice about where they went. And he didn't mind staying in the Farworlder Palace a while longer. "So this is where you Farworlders lived?"

Not here, but in a different area of this structure.

"Is that what we're going to see?"

No. The adult Farworlder chambers are forbidden to humans.

"Why?"

You . . . wouldn't understand.

Corwin got a sense of a place too delicate and complex for a mermyd to enter without doing damage. "So, where are we going?"

"Here," Nia said, and she went in through an archway decorated with carvings of small Farworlders. Corwin could feel her shock, like a blow to the heart, even before he entered the room after her.

It was a large chamber, bigger than Henwyneb's house. The room was filled with marble pedestals, but many had fallen over and broken. There had been crystal bowls on the pedestals—some remained in place, but many lay shattered on the floor. Some of them still contained bits of shell . . . shells like the one Gobaith had lived in.

Nia hovered in the center of the room, gazing at it all, her fists clenched. "Of course. Ma'el destroyed it all."

Corwin felt a keen sorrow spilling over from Gobaith that almost brought tears to his own eyes. The Farworlder drifted among the broken bowls, gently touching the shells with his tentacles. *My crechemates. They're gone. All gone.*

"This is where . . . the baby Farworlders lived?" Corwin asked gently.

"Yes. This was the nursery. I worked here for a while as a guard. I used to play with all the little ones. . . ." Nia stopped and rubbed her eyes, then reached over and put an arm around Gobaith. "I'm sorry. Maybe we shouldn't have come here. Ma'el didn't even spare the little ones. Didn't dare take the chance that some baby Farworlder might survive to interfere."

Corwin swam up to her and put his hand on her shoulder. "We already knew Ma'el was evil. Why should we be surprised? Maybe we'd better move on. We can't afford to be slowed down by sorrow."

Nia's jaw muscles clenched as she swallowed hard. "Oh, don't worry. This sight won't slow me down. I'll remember it every time I wonder whether we're doing the right thing. After seeing this, I know. Ma'el must be destroyed."

As she and Gobaith swam out of the nursery, Corwin wondered if this greater resolve would make her stronger or more reckless. *I guess I'd better prepare myself for either possibility.*

Nia swam on through the Farworlder Palace, feeling herself grow cold inside. Atlanteans were not taught the way of the warrior, and even in her training to be a nursery guard, Nia had only learned how to firmly keep anyone who didn't belong out. But the land-dwellers knew how to fight. And Nia had learned from watching the land-dwellers in Corwin's world. Those who carried swords thought about duty, not feelings.

I don't like this change in you, Nia, Gobaith sent.

Talk to me about it after Ma'el and Joab are dead, Nia thought back.

By then, your heart may be dead as well.

Then it was a price that had to be paid, she told him.

Nia swam down a passageway whose floor was a flight of marble steps. The Farworlder Palace had been built when Atlantis floated on the surface of the ocean, and therefore still retained structures that had once been useful to its land-dweller residents and visitors. Useless now, other than a reminder of the grandeur that Atlantis had seen in ancient times.

A few more turns, down to a lower level of the Farworlder Palace. Nia stopped at the bottom of the stairs and cautiously peered around the wall. Just off to the right was a familiar marble archway. Carved on the lintel and pillars were images of scribes and scrolls, ink brushes and styluses, papyrus reeds and clay tablets. Nia felt an ache of guilt, remembering how Garun had said that working here had been the best job in Atlantis, where he was always able to read and learn. It wasn't until shortly before his death, when everything had fallen apart, that Nia had realized how right he'd been.

"What's this place?" Corwin asked, also peering around, just above her.

"It's the Archives I told you about," Nia replied. "Where scrolls and books of information are kept."

There was a flash of white, and Nia ducked back inside the corridor. Two guards with long spears had emerged from the Archive archway. She thought she recognized them as two mermyds of the Orca clan who used to work for her family.

Do you think they saw us? Nia received the question from Corwin's mind.

I'm not sure, she answered.

They're coming this way, Gobaith sent. *I'll distract them.* He zoomed out of the corridor and did a little dance in front of the guards' faces. Nia could feel the magic Gobaith was using to cloak himself and trick them. Then he sped away down another passageway, leading the guards away from the Archive.

"Now's our chance," Nia said. An iron gate blocked the entrance under the archway. But Nia had learned enough from Corwin about locks that it was no trouble to use a little energy to spring this one. Closing her eyes, she sent a ghost-copy of her hand, made from her own life-energy, into the lock. She could feel the lock shape with her ghost-fingers and push those parts that needed to move. In a few seconds, it was done. Nia drew the ghost-hand back into her own flesh-hand and pushed the gate open.

"Well done. I'm impressed," Corwin said. "Fenwyck would have loved to have had such a power."

"How nice," Nia said, not smiling. "But I intend to use this power only for good." She swam in, her heart aching a little to see the familiar desks and floor-to-ceiling cabinets that were full of the city's knowledge. *If we succeed,*

Water

this will all be so important. I'm glad Ma'el hasn't ruined this, at least. She headed for a glowing circle of light in the ceiling at the end of the room—a hole into a dry room.

An arm, then two, descended through a grate that covered the hole. Nia could see a mermyd lying on the grate, desperately splashing water onto himself.

Nia looked to where the key for the grate had usually hung on the wall. It wasn't there. Nia went to the lock of the grate and again ghost-pulled with energy until the lock clicked and the grate fell open, spilling the hapless mermyd into the water before her.

The mermyd tilted his head back, mouth open in joy, his gills working furiously, his fish tail languidly waving. Finally he spoke. "Oh, thank you, thank you, whoever you are. I thought I was going to die."

Nia didn't recognize this particular mermyd, and his torn and ragged tunic didn't give any clues about his clan. She noticed wounds across his back and chest. "You're not going to die, not if I can help it."

"Thank you, thank—who are you?"

"I am Niniane of the Bluefin clan."

The mermyd's mouth gaped open. He had clearly heard of her. "You . . . you . . ."

"Take it easy. It'll be all right, I hope." Nia reached out her hand to pat his shoulder. He noticed the mark on her palm.

"You became an Avatar, after all!"

"Um, yes, I am."

The mermyd backed away from her and looked wildly around. "Where are the guards? There is only one Farworlder left in Atlantis. You must be working for Ma'el."

"No, no! There's another Farworlder, and he's led the guards away. They won't be back for a while. I've come to help you. Please believe me. Are there others up there?"

"Yes, there are five of us."

"How are they doing?"

"Not well."

"I'll go up and take care of them."

"You'll go into a dry room?" The mermyd looked amazed. "You have no idea how awful it is up there."

"Oh, I've seen worse," Nia said with a slight smile at Corwin. Nia went to the hole and, steeling herself for the ordeal, threw her arms over the lip of the hole and pulled herself up. Then she threw a leg over and pulled herself out of the water into the dry room.

She knelt on all fours, gasping and coughing for a few moments, as she switched from gill- to mouth-breathing. The air was stale, thick and heavy with the smell of rotting fish and sweat.

"Nia?" A husky female voice croaked her name.

Nia looked up. The face before her was instantly recognizable, and yet utterly changed from what she'd known. It was Tyra, the woman who'd raised her.

"Mo——" Nia's voice caught in her throat. Tyra looked haggard, her face thin and drawn, her eyes sunken and red. Her dry skin flaked and her fish tail had whole patches of missing scales. Nia hugged her mother gently. "What have they done to you?"

Tyra only shook her head. "How good to see you," she rasped. "I had . . . I had thought you were dead."

Tears flowed from Nia's eyes. "I was so scared you were, too. Oh, Mother, I am so sorry, so sorry."

Tyra patted her back. "We know now you aren't to blame. Ma'el boasted about how easy it was to fool the councils. To make them believe you were the danger."

Nia glanced around behind Tyra, then frowned. "Where's Pontus, Mother? Was he imprisoned somewhere else?"

Tyra pulled back, gripping Nia's shoulders. "He's dead, Nia. He died in the first assault at the Naming."

Nia hung her head. She had never been happy with her stepfather, even before she'd known he was her stepfather. Still, she never would have wished that on him.

Tyra shook Nia's shoulder. "You've got to get out of

here. Ma'el will imprison or kill you if he finds you. You've got to get away!"

"No, Mother. I've been out in the wide sea, and I've come back. I'm going to save Atlantis, if I can."

"By yourself? No, Nia, you have no idea how powerful Ma'el has become!"

"Oh yes I do. Ma'el has already tried to destroy me several times and failed. And I'm not alone. I've brought help."

At just that moment, Corwin popped his head up through the hole with a splash and said loudly, "Is everyone all right?"

Nia understood him but, of course, her mother didn't. "That's your help?" Tyra rasped. "He's . . . strange-looking. Where are his fins and scales?"

"It's all right, Mother. He's really very nice and very helpful. Gobaith says he makes an excellent Avatar. For a land-dweller."

Corwin held up his hand, the one with the sun-shaped mark, and waved.

The astonishment on her foster mother's face was priceless.

Chapter Seven

Corwin coughed at the foulness of the air in the dry room. He would have liked to have been more formal in greeting the woman who'd raised Nia, but it didn't seem possible, given the situation. Tyra was still staring at him with round, shocked eyes in a thin face.

"A drylander has become an Avatar? This can't be another one of Ma'el's atrocities, can it?" Tyra demanded.

"No, Mother. This is Corwin. He's my . . . friend."

"You always did have strange taste in friends, Nia."

"Shouldn't we be getting your mother back into the water?" Corwin asked.

Nia cast a worried frown at the water. "What if the guards come back?"

"Then it will be better for her to have her strength, won't it?"

Nia nodded and began to ease her mother toward the hole.

"Why does your friend talk so strangely, dear?"

"Because he's new to our language, Mother. He understands us, but he doesn't speak our tongue yet. Though he could if he tried," Nia added, with a significant glare at Corwin.

"Sorry. I thought I was doing well just by understanding," Corwin grumped. He took hold of Tyra's arm and then her scaly tail and helped the woman slide into the water.

Tyra gasped as she sank through the hole. "Madam, are you all right?" Corwin asked, then tried again in Atlantean, searching for the words from Nia's mind. He wasn't sure he got it right.

"It's wonderful," Tyra said as she drifted down into the water. The first mermyd was waiting below and helped guide her from there.

"Why don't you go down and heal her, Nia? I'll help the others."

Nia nodded, clearly shaken by her mother's condition. She slid into the hole like a seal and gave Corwin a quick kiss on the cheek. "Thank you."

"For what?"

But Nia had already dived down out of earshot.

Corwin shrugged and hauled himself out of the water, amazed at how heavy he suddenly felt. He took a quick glance around. There were several cabinets—one tall, one short, one high on the wall. There was something that resembled a chair, bolted to the floor, next to a desk. In between these furnishings, there were three other mermyds lying on the floor against the walls of the room, one an older male and two female mermyds. They were all in as bad condition as Nia's foster mother. They stared back at him with empty, hopeless eyes.

Corwin spoke to them gently, showing them the mark on his palm. He didn't know if he was saying the right words yet, but the action seemed to give the mermyds heart. They were able to summon enough energy to be helped into the water as well.

Corwin slipped down into the water as he eased the last one in. The water felt pleasantly cool on his skin. *No wonder they act like they've reached paradise once they're back in the sea. For them, it's torment to be without the water.* For the first time he realized how hard it must have been for Nia to be on land, even as half land-dweller.

Corwin swam over to Nia. She was holding her hands over Tyra's face and concentrating. "Will she be okay?" Corwin asked when Nia pulled back.

"Yes," Nia answered. "We heal very quickly in water."

"I've noticed. How long have they been in there?"

"Two weeks at least," Nia replied.

Corwin would have whistled, but he wasn't sure he could, underwater. He and Nia went to the other mermyds and did what healing they could for them. As they worked, Corwin asked, "Why are there furnishings up there? What's that room used for?"

"It was secure storage for special documents of the High and Low Councils. It's easier to preserve writing in dry air, so important things would be copied and stored there. This is where I learned about the prophecy that made the council choose Garun to compete in the Trials, instead of me."

Corwin nodded. "When we're done with these people, I want to go back and have another look around," he said.

Nia paused. "Corwin, I know you're excited about learning more, but——"

"No! Not just for my curiosity. I think there might be something up there that could help us."

"You mean the you-know——"

"No, not that," Corwin cut her off again. "A map."

"A . . . map?"

Corwin looked at Nia and realized she'd probably never seen one. Corwin had only seen a few in his lifetime. But Fenwyck had impressed upon him their value. Sea pilot charts were jealously guarded and worth a fortune.

Land-ownership maps were excellent for blackmail. And military maps were worth a king's ransom to the right side, but worth your head if the wrong person discovered you were carrying them. A map could give you godlike knowledge if you understood how to use it.

"It's a drawing of where everything is located," he explained. "All the streets and buildings and everything, in relation to one another. You can figure out the best route to where you want to go, or where something is likely to be. Maybe we could learn exactly where Ma'el has put his fortress, and the best way to get into it."

"That sounds like it would be a big help," Nia said, "but I don't know if any maps exist of Atlantis. Everyone knows where they need to go and drawings are hard to make and use underwater."

"But it's worth a look, isn't it?" he pressed. "Just in case? I'll bet there's something here if we knew where to find it."

Nia nodded. "I've come to trust your bets, Corwin." She turned to Tyra and said, "We're going back into the dry room. Please watch for the guards for us?"

"Yes, of course," Tyra replied, looking back and forth between Nia and Corwin with awe. "You are so brave, both of you."

"We do what we must," Corwin said, holding his head high.

Both Nia and Tyra tilted their heads and regarded him as though he'd just sprouted a new head.

Corwin, you just said "We do brush the fish," Nia informed him telepathically.

"Oh." Corwin felt himself turning a little red. "I haven't quite got the hang of Atlantean yet. Sorry."

Tyra somehow managed to wince and smile at the same time.

"It'll come to you," Nia said. "Let's go up."

Corwin swam to the hole and hauled himself out of the water, disliking it even more than the last time. "What's happening to me?" he muttered after a fit of coughing. "Will I ever be able to return to land?"

"It's just a matter of adjusting," Nia assured him. "I was afraid at one point that I wouldn't be able to return to the sea, but I've been fine."

"That's good to hear," Corwin said. He stood and noted each of the cabinets. "If I were a map, where would I be hiding?"

Nia pointed toward the tallest cabinet. "That's where the finished documents go, the ones that've been sealed against dampness. The desk is for work in progress.

There's nothing on it now. I've never looked in that lower cabinet. Or that high one."

"Is there any rhyme or reason for how the documents are kept?" Corwin asked. "We don't want to spend too long at this."

"There was a code," Nia replied, frowning. "Ma'el gave me the code I needed to find that one document. In there." She pointed to the tall cabinet nearest the exit hole.

"*Ma'el* gave you the code to find that?"

"It's . . . a long story. But it wouldn't help us now anyway."

"Hmm. Then we'll have to use the brute force method." Corwin went to the tall cabinet and opened it. "It wasn't locked?"

Nia shrugged. "This is a dry room. No sane mermyd wants to come into a dry room. That plus the grate is usually lock enough, I guess."

The cabinet had trays filled with flat pieces of papyrus or parchment that had been coated with some hard, clear material. Corwin couldn't read the writing at all. *Maybe it's just as well. I won't be distracted.* He shuffled through the first tray and then the second. Nothing that looked like a map. He went to the bottom-most tray and found no maps there, either.

Nia started to tap her foot with impatience. Her arms

were wrapped around herself. "I'm going to go see how my mother and the others are doing," she said. "Let me know if you find something." She dove back into the water.

"But I can't read any of this!" Corwin protested to her departing feet. *Well, I guess I can't blame her, considering how awful this room is for mermyds. And if I'd had a guardian who'd been tortured, I'd want to look after her, too.* Then Corwin remembered running away as Fenwyck was caught. He winced with guilt. Frustrated, he slammed the tall cabinet shut and went to the low cabinet beside the desk.

This cabinet held documents that weren't coated with the hard material. *Maybe they aren't as important,* Corwin thought. A quick riffling through showed no maps. *Maybe this was a stupid idea,* he thought. *Maybe Nia was right and Atlanteans just don't use maps.*

Corwin went to the last cabinet, the one high up on the wall. Standing on his toes, he was able to open it. Large papers hung in this cabinet vertically, draped over brass rods. These were also coated, but with a more supple material. Corwin, past caring, began pulling all of them down, letting them float to the floor. A couple of them fell into the entry hole.

Then, at the back of the cabinet, he found what he was looking for. "Aha!"

Nia came up sputtering in the hole behind him. "Corwin, what are you doing?" she cried. "These are valuable! Do you have any idea how old they are? You can't just throw them around!"

"If we don't save Atlantis, there's no point to saving the documents, is there? But look at this!" Corwin brought down three papers and spread them out on the floor. Two of them were clearly maps of the city, but at different levels. The third one was a map of a different place.

Nia pushed herself up, dripping, and tried to gather and neatly pile the papers that Corwin had tossed down.

"We don't have time for tidiness!" Corwin snapped. "Come help me decipher these."

Nia crawled over to him. "I'm sorry. I just hate to see so much more lost," she said wistfully before turning her attention to the maps.

"This looks like the part of the city we've seen," Corwin said, pointing to something on one of the maps. "This big circle in the center is the Farworlder Palace, right?"

"Yes, that's what the writing in the corner says. And we should be about . . . here." Nia placed her finger near the edge of the circle.

"So what's this map?" Corwin slid the second one over

the first. "This looks like the city, too, but it's different. Is it older?"

"No." Nia peered at it for a moment, and then her face lit up. "No, this is the Lower Depths! See, here are the filtration tubes, and here are the oxygenation tunnels. This is the hunters'/fishers' market we passed. This area is where the works are that keep the city warm and the water moving. And this is where those Sunfish guards said Ma'el was living."

"Now the trick," Corwin began, "is to look for a place on this map that would appeal to evil tyrants like Ma'el and Joab."

"Well," Nia said. "He would want to be near the controls of the city. And look over here—" She pointed at a large, empty area of the city map. "This isn't marked as anything. And it only has these two entries."

"A perfect headquarters," Corwin murmured. "Could you find this area now, when we need to?"

"Easily," Nia said. "It's on the opposite side of the city from the filtration tube we entered. And if we look at these two maps . . ." She held up the first one and then flipped to the second. "The best way down to that area is an access tunnel that leads from over here, the Orca Palace . . . hmmm."

"Why hmmmm?"

"The Orcas were a clan of powerful palace guardians. If they've survived, as the Sunfish have, then we'll have a tough time getting by them."

"And it would be in Ma'el's interest to let them survive."

"Probably."

"You're back to your bad habit of being the mistress of bad news."

"I'm afraid so. Want to hear worse?"

"No."

"I'll tell you anyway. Ma'el definitely has the you-know-what. One of the mermyds we've just rescued, Theron, has seen it. He heard Ma'el ordering a servant to store it away. Apparently Ma'el was worried it might be a symbol to rally rebellion."

"Well, that could be good for us, if we can find it," Corwin said. "We could use all the rallying relics we can get."

"That was the official story. But Theron thinks Ma'el was angry. Maybe he'd tried to use it but failed."

"That's even better," Corwin said. "If the you-know-what was made for peace, then of course it wouldn't work for Ma'el. But hopefully it will for us."

"Yes, but it can't help us while it's hidden in his stronghold," Nia pointed out. "If we're caught before we can find it, then everything's lost."

Corwin had to laugh. "You're outdoing yourself today, Lady-Prophetess-of-Doom Nia. Is it time to give up and head back to Wales?"

"I'm no less determined to fight Ma'el, Corwin. But we need to know what we're up against. We can't afford to be careless."

"You have no idea how reassured I am to hear you say that."

"That includes not flinging papers around so that Ma'el knows where we've been and what we've seen."

"Oh." Corwin looked around at the mess in the dry room. He decided he'd better change the subject fast. "What about this?" he asked, pulling out the third map. "What's this a map of?" Nia peered at it. "Oh—it's a map of the dry-lander world, Corwin. We're taught this in Academy. Around this sea was where all the ancient kingdoms lay that Atlantis used to trade with. These islands are Hellenica. Along this river lay Egypt. In the middle of this leglike thing is Roma. Way up here in this corner, this island is Britannia."

"That's my home!" Corwin said. "Some people called my land Britannia," he explained.

"So *that's* where we were," Nia mused. "All the way up there."

Corwin stared at it as if he should be able to see the

hills and rocky shores within the bare outline. It seemed very small compared with the rest of the world. Corwin began to understand how little he'd seen in his life. How little about the world he'd known. Henwyneb, for all his sightlessness, had "seen" more, just from the stories he'd gathered from his guests.

"But what are these circles and lines connecting them?"

"Wait, it explains down here." Nia silently read a block of text in a corner of the parchment. "Ah! These are the locations of the centers of power. Remember Gobaith told us about them? The centers are located in places where the Earth's energies tap directly into the unis, this says. And look—there's one here, in your homeland, Corwin. That must be the shrine we found."

Corwin looked at the symbols beside the circle where Nia was pointing. "Yes, those were carved on the walls of the ruin. If we'd known how to use their power, we might have been able to save ourselves a lot of trouble. We might have been able to destroy or at least weaken Ma'el before coming to Atlantis."

"But we didn't," Nia said. "And this map doesn't explain how they were to be used. Maybe only a Farworlder would know. Down here, someone has added a notation: 'The centers of power were ordered destroyed when Atlantis sank, to avoid misuse by the land-dwellers.' But the one in your country wasn't completely destroyed, just buried."

"Maybe your ancestors just didn't get around to that one," Corwin said with a shrug. "It's farthest away from the others. Maybe they felt my people would be too stupid to figure out what it was for."

"I doubt that," Nia said.

"Well, this map is interesting, but it doesn't help us much now," Corwin said. "I'll fold up the city maps and bring those along."

"Let's pick up the rest of these and hide them somewhere," Nia suggested.

There was a bubbling and splashing in the hole behind them. The young merman they had first rescued appeared and shook the water off of his face. "Forgive my intrusion, Avatar Nia, Avatar Corwin, but the guards have been seen and they're returning this way. With them is a Farworlder whom we assume is your joined king, but the guards are ignoring him. We're going to find places to hide."

Nia paused a moment. "Very well. Thank you."

The mermyd dove below again.

"I guess we'd better leave, too," Nia said. "Oh, but these papers . . . how do we hide them?"

"Why bother?" Corwin asked. "Ma'el's not going to

care. He'll already know we've been here. Let's just go!"

"Okay," Nia said, a little reluctantly. "Corwin, did you hear what he called us?"

Corwin looked at her. "Yes—he called us Avatars. I guess it is a little strange, hearing someone say that to me. But isn't it normal for you? You've known all along that's what you are down here."

"It was the tone in his voice," she replied. "No one's ever spoken to me with that kind of . . . respect? Awe?"

"Well, don't let it go to your head," Corwin said, pushing papers out of the way. "That's what turns kings into tyrants."

"I'll try to remember that," Nia said with a slight smile, and she dove back in through the hole.

Corwin folded the city maps and tucked them into his tunic. Instinctively taking a few deep breaths, even though he didn't need to, he dove in after Nia.

Nia swam to her mother, who was emerging from her hiding spot beneath a desk. Tyra was already looking better. "I'm sorry, Avatar Nia. We can't stay here."

"It's all right," Nia said. Then she paused. "Mother, you don't have to call me Avatar," she said, taking both of Tyra's hands.

Tyra smiled. "I want to. To show how proud I am of you. And to convince myself that there's still hope for Atlantis. Now you and your friend must come with me. I know some cellars in the Bluefin Palace we could escape to, where you can plan your rebellion."

Nia shook her head. "We don't have time to hide, Mother. Ma'el knows we're here, and we have to try to stop him before he has a chance to root us out. We have to keep ahead of him."

"You're going to just fight him outright, by yourselves?" Tyra asked in horror. "But how can you? You're . . . you're so young!"

Nia held up her right hand and showed her mother the sun-shaped mark. "It's our duty to try. And if we can't, who else can?"

Tyra nodded and hugged her. "I understand. Good luck to you. Take care, Avatar Nia. I—I love you."

After a pause to sort through her conflicting feelings, Nia replied, "I love you, too."

"Avatar Nia," said the young male mermyd, "I am Gyes. Let me serve you. I know where many of the other dry rooms are. If it will assist your plans, I will free as many as I can."

Nia nodded. "Thank you, Gyes. If we can keep Ma'el

distracted with many problems in the city, he may not notice when we slip into his stronghold."

"It would help," Gyes said, "if your Farworlder king could come with me. Many might be healed by him."

"I'm sorry," Nia said, "but we can't do that. It could be dangerous if we were separated."

Gyes nodded with acceptance. "I'll do the best I can, then, without."

"Avatar Nia," said a young woman mermyd with light brown hair, and a tail of white and brown scales. "I am Eldoris. I was a servant in Ma'el's stronghold. I was arrested for stealing food for my family, who were hiding. I know where the sword you're searching for might be. I can help guide you."

"That's a brave offer," Nia said, "but it would be very risky for you."

Eldoris shook her head and gazed at the floor. "Ma'el had my family found and killed. We were the last of the Skate clan. I will do all I can to help avenge them."

Nia placed a hand on Eldoris's shoulder. "Then I thank you for your help. But don't let your hunger for vengeance make you careless."

"I won't, Avatar," she replied.

"Avatar Nia," said the older male mermyd, "I, Theron,

have spent all my life among the waterworks of the lower depths. If you think it will help, I will do damage to some of the conduits in order to create further distraction."

Nia nodded. "That might be good, Theron, but don't do anything that will immediately endanger our people. There are few of us enough as it is."

Theron bowed. "As you will, Avatar."

Nia blinked at the solemn words directed at her, her heart filling with new emotions. She saw the hope on these mermyds' faces and marveled at their open adulation. She'd been just an ordinary Atlantean girl a month ago. In Corwin's land she'd been treated like a child, like a freak, by all the land-dwellers except Henwyneb. Now her spirit swelled with strength, as if the belief the mermyds had in her was passed on to her, giving her power in some mystical fashion. She deeply wanted to be the rescuer everyone hoped for. But Nia also felt an edge of fear that she might disappoint them, that she might instead bring their destruction—just like the old prophecy had originally warned.

Gobaith sped in through the archway. *I've trapped the guards behind a fallen screen, but they'll escape from behind that quickly. We must leave. Hurry!*

The mermyds stared at Gobaith with wide-eyed reverence.

"Our king says we must hurry and depart," Nia said briskly. "Try to be brave. Atlantis has survived for thousands of years. We will survive the outrage of Ma'el as well."

"Hail and good fortune to you, Avatar Nia, Avatar Corwin," said the mermyds.

"Hail and good fortune to you, glowing sea-snails," Corwin said in return, clearly still having trouble speaking Atlantean.

The other mermyds simply smiled in tolerant bafflement and said, "To the glowing sea-snails!"

With a last hug for her mother, Nia said good-bye. Letting Eldoris guide them, Nia, Corwin and Gobaith left the Archives.

"Maybe from now on you'd better let me do the talking," Nia said softly to Corwin.

"What? What'd I say?"

"Nothing too embarrassing. Yet."

"But *they* liked it."

"You called them 'glowing sea-snails.'"

"Oh. I hope that's not an insult."

"No, but sometime——"

"Sometime I might say something insulting. Got it. Shutting up now, Avatar Nia."

"Don't call me that."

"Why not? Everyone else does."

"That's why not."

Eldoris looked back at them. "If you please, good Avatars, let's all be silent from here on."

Eldoris led them through dim, deserted colonnades and corridors, some occasionally sloping down. Nia hadn't explored the Farworlder Palace much beyond the nursery and the Archives. The fear of getting lost and accidentally finding herself in the forbidden areas had stopped her. Now she didn't know where they were and had lost her frame of reference. Worse yet, the water became darker as they moved away from lighted areas, and it was becoming more difficult to see. They seemed to be heading in the right direction, according to her directional sense, but ultimately she had to trust Eldoris.

They left the Farworlder Palace through a small, undistinguished archway and entered a side street at street-level. Nia or Corwin could have put down their legs and walked, if they chose, but it was much faster and more comfortable to swim.

Finally Eldoris stopped, treading water with her tail. She nodded toward something ahead and said, "There's the entrance. But we have to hide here a moment."

Nia, Corwin, Gobaith and Eldoris lined up along the

edge of one building. When Nia peered around the corner, she could dimly see a dark archway, flanked by two mermyd guards. The guards had retained their Orca livery of black and white, and they held long spears in their hands. These were not the idle, for-show Orca guardsmen that would keep the unwanted out of noble parties in past times. These two looked tough and determined. *And,* Nia thought grimly, *Ma'el must have sent them there just to wait for us*.

Chapter Eight

"So, what are we waiting for?" Corwin asked softly, as Nia peered around the corner again. "Let Gobaith do his little dance to get them out of the way, and we'll move on."

"It's not that simple," Nia said. "These mermyds are expecting us."

"Let's see. We've scared off the King of Britain and his knights and his wizards. I've thrown Ma'el and Joab themselves over a castle wall. We've defeated a horde of hungry sharks, a whirlpool and the kraken. Gobaith has led two sets of Atlantean guards off on merry chases. How difficult can *these* guards be?"

"That's not the point," Nia argued. "We're closer to Ma'el's lair now. And these mermyds won't be overawed by Gobaith. Somehow we have to sneak past them without giving them any reason to worry."

"Ah! Sneaking," Corwin said. "Now *that's* my sort of

challenge. None of this risk-your-neck, knock-down drag-out fighting business for a change."

"Shhh!" Nia hissed. "They're looking this way."

Corwin kept his mouth shut and tried to let his thieving instincts take over. Nothing came to mind right away. Usually, if Fenwyck had a bit of larceny in mind, going in under the noses of two well-trained guards wouldn't be the route he'd choose. There was always a window or side door that would be a safer entrance.

"Are you sure," Corwin asked Eldoris, careful to choose the right words from Nia's mind before speaking, "that this is the only way we can go in?"

Eldoris shrugged. "It's the way I know."

"We don't have time to search for another," Nia said.

Do you have any ideas? Corwin mentally asked Gobaith.

You're the clever one, replied the Farworlder. *We're counting on you.*

Can't you just wave your tentacles and do some magic ju-ju so that they won't see us or something?

I'm tired after all the so-called 'dancing' for the guards. And why do I have to do all the magic for us? You're an Avatar. It's your turn.

Corwin sighed. *My turn. Wonderful. I hate having to be clever under pressure.* But life with Fenwyck had demanded precisely that. At least the beachcomber life had been peaceful. Until he'd found the leviathan and the shell that had contained Gobaith.

Corwin rubbed his forehead as if to stimulate thought. *If the guards are waiting for us, then they need to be distracted by something as not us as possible. Something they might expect to see, but not us. But if they've been ordered to wait only for us, then they won't even bother with something not us. Unless it was something more important than us. This is ridiculous.*

"We need to distract them in a nonfrightening way," he murmured. Fenwyck had known lots of techniques for distraction. It was half of the art of stage magic, after all. What would be pleasantly distracting? Well, a girl, but that was too obvious, and too risky for Nia or Eldoris. Corwin remembered a toy used by Fenwyck once, a spinning top with swirly lines on it. Fenwyck had been able to keep an audience member quite fascinated with it, long enough for it to be . . . profitable. But Corwin had no such toy.

Then Corwin remembered the glowing jellyfish he had seen when he, Nia and Gobaith had first arrived in the Great Deep. The gently pulsating, drifting, dancing creature had been fascinating. Corwin could have watched it for hours if their mission hadn't been so urgent. *The guards must be bored if they've been waiting for a long time. Maybe a sight like that would be just soothing enough. And a jellyfish wouldn't be that unusual here.*

Corwin whipped off the white tunic he wore, catching the tube holding the maps and handing it to Nia. "Hold these, please. Gobaith, here." Corwin draped the tunic over Gobaith's head, so that just the tentacles showed beneath. "Gobaith, you're a jellyfish. Think like a jellyfish. Dance like a jellyfish. Convince the guards out there that you are, indeed, a jellyfish. I'll do an illusion spell to make you glow like one. You must entrance the guards. Beguile them. And try to get them to step away from the arch, while you're at it."

Don't ask much, do you?

"I have great faith in you, Gobaith."

Corwin put his hands on the Farworlder's cloth-covered head and concentrated on the memory of the jellyfish he had seen. Energy glowed beneath his hands and spread through the cloth. It poofed up and spread outward like the mantle of the creature Corwin had seen. Lines of tiny, glimmerimg lights appeared on Gobaith's tentacles.

"That's almost right," Nia said. "Here." She also placed her hands on the billowing cloth mantle and suddenly

Gobaith's disguise had a translucent quality, as though you could see all the way through.

"Beautiful!" Corwin said. "Now you're ready. Go out and dazzle your awaiting public, Gobaith."

Corwin could swear the Farworlder uttered a mental sigh before drifting out from behind the building and slowly pulsing toward the Orca guards.

As Corwin and Nia watched, Gobaith began his act. Bounce, drift, bounce, spin, float up, sink down: Gobaith did a mesmerizing dance. Corwin had to be careful not to watch too closely, or he'd be entranced himself.

The Orca guards looked puzzled at first. Then they began to gently smile as they watched Gobaith. But they didn't move away from the arch.

Great, Corwin thought. *Now what?*

I'm going to have to move in closer, Gobaith sent. *And you all will have to do something risky. I will try to hold their gaze at a high eye-level. You will have to crawl between them while they're looking up.*

Don't ask much, do you? Corwin thought.

I have great faith in you, Gobaith replied. *I'm going to move in now. Wait for my go-ahead. Explain the plan to Eldoris, Nia.*

Nia began speaking softly to Eldoris, while Gobaith

drifted closer to the guards, but higher, so that their faces were tilted up. Then Gobaith began to spin, flashing lights along his "mantle" at a fast but regular, pulsing rhythm. The guards stared wide-eyed, their mouths going slack.

Now! Gobaith sent.

"I'll go first," Nia volunteered, "to show Eldoris how to do it." Nia kicked off and built up speed crossing the roadway at about knee-level to the guards. Just before she reached them, she stretched her arms ahead and her legs straight back and arrowed between the guards in a perfect motion.

"Well, that doesn't look too hard," Corwin murmured. "You next," he told Eldoris, nudging her gently. Looking frightened but determined, Eldoris swam forward. She had a tail rather than legs like Nia, but she put the tail to good use to gain momentum. At the last moment, she turned sideways, also knifing between the guards without their noticing.

"My turn," Corwin said to himself.

Hurry, Gobaith sent. *I'm getting dizzy.*

Corwin pushed off from the building corner and skimmed along the roadway. But he let one knee bend too far and it banged against a flagstone. Corwin silently mouthed an "Ow!" as he rolled over and held his aching leg. He wondered if he had time to heal himself. Or maybe transform his legs into a tail like Eldoris had.

HURRY!

So much for that idea. Corwin gritted his teeth and ran like a merdog on fingers and toes toward the guards. As he got closer and closer, he realized he didn't have the speed to neatly pass between the Orcas and besides, he was bigger than either Nia or Eldoris. His odds weren't looking good. *What do I do, Gobaith?*

Just get past them as fast as you can! Gobaith began to sway from side to side, and the guards' attention swayed with him. *Go!*

Corwin leapt. His arms, his chest, his hips went through, but his hurt leg was still bent and it banged against the leg of the righthand guard. *Yipe!*

Go go go go go go!

Corwin swam for all he was worth, ignoring the pain in his knee, ignoring the yelling of the guards behind him. *I've done it now. All my cleverness for nothing. We're through.* Down and down he swam, until he came out the other end of the passage in a dimly lit corridor that was like daylight compared to the place he'd just left. He plowed into Nia. "Go! The guards are right behind me!"

No, they're not. Gobaith shot out of the passage over Corwin's head. *I convinced them that they bumped into each other. They're now busily accusing one another of clumsiness. A good thing they weren't friends much to begin with.*

Corwin let out a long, bubbling sigh of relief and let go of Nia with embarrassment. "Thank you, Gobaith. I owe you one."

I owe you many. There's no need for accounting between us.

Nia gently pushed Corwin off of her. "Quiet, now. Eldoris told me that servants of Ma'el come along here frequently. We have to pretend to be good little slaves."

"How can I do that? Gobaith left my tunic behind."

"It didn't fit you anyway," Nia said. "But Eldoris will help us," Nia nodded to Eldoris.

Eldoris nodded back and closed her eyes. As they watched, her hair darkened to almost Callimar's color, and her tail scales became gray and moss green.

"Does she have an oculus?" whispered Corwin.

"No, this is a skill all of her family has . . . had. They can change color at will to match their surroundings. It's probably why Ma'el wanted to destroy them—they're potentially dangerous."

"I'll be right back," Eldoris said. "Wait here." And she swam off.

"Are you sure we can trust her?" Corwin asked.

Nia shrugged. "I do. The Skate clan was known for humility and strict honesty, so that they wouldn't abuse their powers of deception. Otherwise they wouldn't have survived as long as they did."

Before long, Eldoris returned, holding a large handled basket and a new tunic for Corwin, with long sleeves. Corwin put the tunic on. "At least this one fits," he said.

"And with the sleeves," Nia added, "no one will notice the hair on your arms."

I guess the basket's for me, Gobaith sent.

"I'm afraid so," Nia said with a rueful smile. "Dignity is something we can't afford right now."

Gobaith swam over to the basket and as Nia held open the lid, he curled up inside it. *It's not nearly as cozy as my shell was. I'm almost getting too big for this.*

"You'll just have to make do." Nia closed the lid. With Eldoris's help, Nia did up her long, silvery hair in a knot on her head, and Eldoris covered it with a dark scarf. Then Nia shut her eyes and concentrated hard. Though it hurt, she used her powers to make her nose just a little flatter and broader, her eyes a darker blue, and to put a bit of fin on her ears. When she opened her eyes again, Corwin was staring at her.

"What?" Nia asked.

"No, you just—you look different."

Nia scowled. "Do I look different enough that I won't be recognized?"

"Well, I wouldn't have if I didn't know you before."

"Good," Nia said. "You know, if I'd had this ability before . . . everything, I might have made myself completely different. I was so unhappy with my appearance, I'd probably have made myself look like Callimar."

"I'm glad you didn't," Corwin said in a funny voice. "I like the way you are. Were."

Nia blushed and glanced away. "I'll change back when it's all over. Thank you."

"Should we do anything transformational for me?" Corwin asked. "No, wait, it'll hurt, won't it? Maybe I'll just be fine the way I am."

"Hmmm," Nia said, "you should at least put fins on your ears, and maybe make your nose a little bigger."

Corwin winced. "I was afraid you'd say that." He put his hands to his nose, saying "Ooh! Ow! Oo!" And then he put his hands to his ears and stretched out little fins on them. "How do I look?"

"Definitely different."

"Handsome-different or ugly-different?"

"Honored Avatars, we'd better go," Eldoris interrupted,

glancing back over her shoulder. "The servant shift is about to change."

"Gobaith," Nia said, tapping the basket, "can you take a look ahead in time and tell us what we should watch for?"

I have tried, he sent back. *But my future vision is clouded. Something is preventing me from understanding clearly what lies ahead.*

"Probably Ma'el's doing," Nia said. "He managed the same thing while he was plotting to take over Atlantis. That's why the High and Low Councils became confused and didn't know what to do. That's why they blamed me." Nia put aside her bitterness and followed behind Eldoris. Corwin joined her.

"I hate going in blind like this," he muttered.

"What choice do we have?" Nia asked.

They swam into a much more brightly lit corridor in which many mermyds came and went. Nia kept her head down, trying to copy the expressions of fear and exhaustion that were on the other mermyds' faces. She didn't look too closely at anyone, afraid she might recognize someone and give herself away.

A gate loomed ahead, but it stood open to allow the streams of mermyds to move through. There was an Orca guard beside it, but he looked bored and made no effort to stop anyone. The three of them easily swam through the gate and into Ma'el's stronghold.

Whatever Nia had been expecting, this wasn't it. The gate opened up into a huge room with water much warmer than that in the rest of Atlantis, and light much brighter. It was like the tide-pool garden that her father Dyonis had tended, only on a much grander scale. There were anemones in wild colors and sea ferns and living coral. There were bright-colored fish darting in and out of artfully sculpted rocks. The floor wasn't finished paving-stone, but instead the rough rock of the seabed itself.

"Lord Ma'el wants us to get used to living closer to the surface," Eldoris explained. "He's even told Atlanteans that he's going to insist on long-term dry-room living for everyone, especially children, so that we'll be ready when Atlantis again rises to the top of the sea."

How nice, Nia thought darkly. *Ma'el's going to make Atlanteans suffer for his grandiose plans.* She was sure he hadn't asked the populace of Atlantis for their vote on the matter.

Eldoris led them off to the right, away from the gardens and toward a barer, emptier part of the great compound.

"Can you show us where the sword is?" Nia asked softly.

"Yes," Eldoris whispered back. "Follow me closely."

The water began to taste more minerally, and Nia knew they were getting close to the rift vents. The passageways they entered were similar to those near the filtration tubes, except more mermyds swam by. Nia had the feeling they were getting closer to the control area of the works themselves, closer to where Ma'el might be. But she didn't risk saying anything to Eldoris, in case they'd be overheard.

"Here," Eldoris finally said. They had come to a tall door with a scallop-shaped knob. Eldoris waited until there were no mermyds nearby and then opened the door. "Go in. Quickly."

Nia and Corwin swam in. *Is it here?* Gobaith asked from the basket. *I feel a vague presence.*

Wait while we look around. Nia let her eyes adjust to the dimmer light in the storage room. It was filled with stacks of rich furnishings, tables of ebony, ivory tusks and animal horns, clamshell chairs, land-dweller statues from sunken ships, piles of gold land-dweller coins, sealed jars containing wine and dates and who-knew-what from long ago and far away.

"I've never seen wealth like this," Corwin said in awe.

"And it's all useless here," Nia said. "Although I guess Ma'el thinks it will help him for trade once Atlantis surfaces."

"Look, swords!"

Nia followed Corwin's pointing hand. Beside the wall to their right was a heap of scattered swords and shields.

"But those are from a land-dweller ship, Corwin."

"Yes, but where better to hide a special sword than in plain sight?" Nia stared back at him in confusion. "Oh, right—you've never had to hide any stol—um, any misplaced items. Just trust me on this, okay?"

Nia sighed and swam to the pile of weaponry. Taking up one short sword in hand, Nia poked through the pile.

Can you sense it? Gobaith asked.

Nia did sense a curious itching in the back of her mind. She relaxed and closed her eyes, letting her hands dig wherever they felt guided to.

There it is!

Nia opened her eyes. And then she saw part of the hilt gleaming brighter than the other swords, sticking out from the pile. She carefully lifted off the weapons that lay on top of it. Eikis Calli Werr, its silvery blade shimmering, a faint glow coming from the hilt where the oculus lay. "I had forgotten how beautiful you are," Nia said softly. She reached out to grasp it.

There was a discreet cough at the door.

"Just a little longer, Eldoris," Nia said. And then she turned. It wasn't Eldoris.

A tall, thin mermyd hovered at the door, his narrow black fish tail twitching. "May I ask what you two are doing in here?" he said officiously.

Nia vaguely remembered him as being of the Remora clan. Remoras were known for their service and discretion. Of course Ma'el would want them working for him. As humbly as possible, Nia replied, "We were ordered to tidy this room up, sir. We meant no trouble."

The Remora's eyes narrowed. "I don't recall seeing either of you before. You're new here, aren't you?"

"Yes, yes, we're new." Nia bobbed her head, and Corwin followed her lead.

The Remora sighed. "No one tells me anything. Very well, come with me."

"But—but we haven't finished our task, sir."

"You may come back to it later. My orders are to bring all new hires to the central office for inspection and orientation. It was Eldoris who brought you in?"

Nia's heart thudded and she swallowed hard. She didn't want to betray her fellow rebel who'd already risked so much.

Say yes, Gobaith advised her. *It's the answer he is expecting.*

With a heavy heart, Nia said, "Yes. It was Eldoris."

"Fine," said the Remora. "She will be given proper credit for her recruitment. Follow me."

Nia blinked. Feeling just a little relieved, she lowered her head and folded her hands in an attitude of servitude. Corwin did the same, but Nia could see in his eyes that he resented it. They both followed meekly after the Remora.

"Where are we going?" Corwin asked in his language.

"To someplace where we'll be officially enrolled as workers, I guess. It could be useful for our disguise."

"What about . . . the you-know-what?"

"We'll come back for it later. Now shhh."

The Remora looked back over his shoulder at them. "Why is that fellow speaking gibberish?"

Nia winced. "It's a childhood language we spoke when we were small. My brother's anxious at being in the great Lord Ma'el's household. It soothes him to speak in our old code, that's all."

The Remora rolled his eyes. "Well, we are all different, I suppose."

Nia blew out through her gills in relief.

The Remora continued to lead them deeper among the works. Huge pipes lined the walls and ceilings of the corridors, and the water throbbed with the power of the engines that drove the circulatory system of the city. Finally, he opened a circular hatch, much like the hatch on the filtration tube. "In here," he instructed.

Nia and Corwin swam inside.

The hatch boomed shut behind them.

A huge brass pillar rose in the center of the room. Knobs and levers stuck out from it, making it appear like a mutated tree. Then out from behind the pillar swam a bizarre-looking mermyd. His arms and torso were covered with a bony plate armor, like fish scales of enormous size. He had two short, muscular legs, as well as a fish tail sticking out from his lower back. His face was hidden behind a mask made from a king crab's carapace. And then he spoke.

"Welcome, my friends! I'm so glad you made it here at last!"

It was Ma'el.

Chapter Nine

"We were betrayed," Corwin said, balling his fists.

"Oh, don't blame sweet Eldoris," Ma'el said. "She just knows where her best interests lie. If Eldoris has any hope of keeping the Skate bloodline intact, then she has to stay alive by any means necessary. Even if it means spying for me in a dry room and escorting the 'last Avatars of Atlantis' into my custody."

Nia said nothing, only glared at Ma'el.

"So overwhelmed you can't speak? I guess I don't blame you."

It worked once, why not again? Corwin thought. He launched himself at Ma'el and began to beat upon the mermyd's arms where he remembered the oculae lay.

Ma'el merely stood there and laughed. "Corwin, do you really think I wouldn't learn from my defeats? This armor I've grown protects me quite well, don't you think?"

Ma'el delivered a powerful punch to Corwin's middle,

driving him back and knocking the air out of him.

Nia raised her arms as if to attempt a spell. She managed to summon energy into her hands, but shrieked as Ma'el lifted his own hands. The water around Nia boiled and she waved her scalded arms and hands frantically.

Corwin tried to contact Gobaith, but the Farworlder wasn't responding. "Stop hurting her!" he cried at last.

"Of course. I only wished to keep the young lady from doing something she would regret."

The water cooled noticeably and Nia backed away, hugging herself and still glaring at Ma'el.

"Be aware, my young friends, that you are in *my* territory now. I have all the advantage here. So I suggest that you behave yourselves."

"Where's your partner in evil, Joab?" Corwin asked, when he could speak again, as he tried to think of what to do.

"Right behind you," Ma'el said coolly.

Corwin whipped around to see the enormous, mottled, dark purple Farworlder. The huge golden eyes stared with malevolent glee at him. Corwin was certain that if Farworlders could smile, Joab would be grinning from eye to eye.

Corwin was about to try to swim away when Joab's tentacles wrapped around his chest and arms. One tentacle slithered around Corwin's neck, holding his gills shut. Up close, Joab seemed even bigger than he'd been at Castle Carmarthen.

I can't breathe! Corwin thought as he struggled hard to get free. But Joab's limbs were like iron bands: immovable.

"No!" Nia cried.

"Stay calm," Ma'el told her. "I'm not going to kill your friend. He has something I need, after all. As do you."

Corwin felt the tentacle around his neck loosen ever so slightly, just enough so that Corwin could pull some water in through his gills. Even so, spots were beginning to form before his eyes and he felt faint.

"Gobaith! Wake up!" Nia yelled, shaking the basket.

"I'm afraid your little charge is incapable of hearing you," Ma'el said. "His mind is wrapped up in a little pocket of the unis, from which it can't escape. Not without our help. Did you think the obstacles I set for you were just for show? Joab and I learned very particularly what all of your strengths and weaknesses are, the three of you. We're very impressed. For such a young Farworlder, Gobaith's skills and talent are highly developed. But he's still very young. I'm sure we will be able to tease Gobaith's secrets out of him with no trouble. Before we kill him and take his oculus. Unless, of course . . . you three would like to pledge fealty to me?"

Corwin was beginning to think that might not be a bad idea, as a delaying tactic at least.

"Never," Nia said.

So much for that, Corwin thought. *We're as good as dead.*

"Unfortunately, that's what I expected," Ma'el said, sounding genuinely upset. "I really didn't want things to turn out like this for us, Nia. But, you know, it's easy to be courageous in comfort. I'll give you a little more time to think—in less pleasant surroundings. You too, young land-dweller."

Joab began to swim toward the hatch door, with the bound-up Corwin in tow. Corwin struggled again, but a tightening of the tentacle around his neck reminded him to behave. Corwin decided to just relax so that he could think.

As the door opened and Joab headed out, Corwin waved the one hand that could move a little at Nia, realizing with a pang that it might be the last time he'd see her. He thought he heard her faint thoughts in his mind, *Be brave. I love you.*

Fears of torment were banished for a moment as the door slammed shut behind them. *Did she just say what I think she said?*

Too bad it didn't look like he'd have a chance to ask her. He could feel the aura of Joab's dark thoughts surrounding him, smothering him, making telepathy impossible with either Nia or Gobaith. Corwin felt as though his soul were being coated with slime. *And I thought King Vortigern and his son were as bad as evil got. They were just stinging ants compared to this creature. Now if he and Ma'el are joined, which of them is the greater evil? Was Ma'el decent before Joab got ahold of his mind? Why do I even care? Does it matter?*

Corwin was carried to a wall made up of little cells, sort of like a honeycomb. With one tentacle, Joab opened the grate that covered one of the cells. Then the Farworlder tightened the tentacle around Corwin's neck.

Hey! Hey! You weren't supposed to kill me yet! Corwin thought desperately until the spots again appeared before his eyes and his body went limp. Just as he knew he was about to black out, Joab flung him into the cell and slammed the grate shut. Blowing air out of his siphons with a chuff-chuff-chuff sound that greatly resembled gloating laughter, Joab swam away.

Corwin lay curled up in his cell, dragging water through his gills and sucking out what oxygen he could. *I wonder if Ma'el keeps this water stale just so his prisoners will stay weak.* His head swimming from the effort of breathing, Corwin drifted off to sleep, exhausted.

When he woke up, Corwin had no idea how much time had passed. He was vaguely hungry. He reached out with his mind to Nia, but couldn't find her. He tried Gobaith too, but was again blocked.

I spent so much time wishing Gobaith and Nia weren't connected to my thoughts, Corwin mused, *and now they're not, and it's the worst loneliness I've ever felt, like part of myself has been cut away.*

Nia said she loved me, he reminded himself. But with a pang of sorrow, he realized that nothing might ever come of that. His life might end within this tiny cell. Its gray stone walls might be the last thing that he saw. It all seemed so unfair.

What's Ma'el waiting for, anyway? Corwin wondered. *Why doesn't he just kill us and get it over with?*

Corwin rolled over, trying to find a comfortable position to curl up in. He tried several and they were all equally awkward. He settled for lying on his right side, knees up to his chest. He stared out through the grate enclosing his cell. All he could see was a gray stone wall on the opposite side of the corridor. There were little bits of shell embedded in the stone. If you gazed at them long enough, they could form patterns like the stars in the night sky.

I wouldn't want to be a king, Corwin thought, his mind

wandering. *All that false adulation and the need to make life-and-death decisions every day. I wouldn't mind advising a king, though. Trying to help a king be sensible about power. Maybe I should have taken that offer by Vortigern's wizards to become one of them.* Corwin thought a little more. *No. Vortigern would have just become upset with me when I couldn't find the enemies he wanted. Some kings you just can't talk sense into.*

Corwin rolled over again to face the far wall of his cell. *Maybe you have to start with a prince.* The sneering face of Prince Vortimer came to mind. *A young prince. One that hasn't been corrupted by the Vortigerns and the Fenwycks of this world. Someone who knows instinctively that if you use power wisely, you can have . . . well, a place like Atlantis used to be. Prosperous and at peace. Of course, you'd have to have soldiers in a land-dweller kingdom. Because there are all those other land-dweller kingdoms that will circle like wolves and attack if they see you've got more wealth than they do. So you'd need knights. But you'd want to pick them carefully. Take the ones who believe in your cause, and wouldn't betray you.*

Corwin sighed. *Why am I even thinking about all this? It'll never happen. I'll be lucky if I live until tomorrow.*

A hooded servant in a white tunic appeared at the

grate and pushed a folded piece of cloth under it. "Your meal." Then the servant hurried away.

"Hey! Hey!" Corwin called, but the servant didn't come back. Corwin unfolded the cloth and found only bits of crabmeat with seaweed wrapped around it. *I don't even know if this is a gourmet meal for an Atlantean, or food for the lowest of the low.* But Corwin ate it, trying to remind himself that it might be the last meal he ever ate. It didn't make the fishy, salty morsels any better. He wished even more that Gobaith could be in his mind, to tell him just how wonderful this should taste.

After eating, Corwin grew tired again, and he drifted back to sleep. He woke up and almost immediately wondered why he was still alive. What did Ma'el have planned for him?

A hooded servant again appeared at the grate and pushed a folded piece of cloth under it. "Your meal."

Already? That seemed fast, even though he wasn't sure exactly how long he'd been napping.

He figured the servant would rush off again, but surprisingly, she didn't. Instead, she stepped closer and pulled back her hood. It was Callimar.

"Calli—"

"Shhh!" Callimar looked all around her, then pressed her

face against the grate. "If we hurry, I can take you to Nia."

"Is she all right?"

"No time to talk." Callimar unlocked the grate to his cell and opened it, beckoning him to come out. He slipped out of the cell as fast as he could.

I don't know if I can trust this creature, he thought. *But I'm better off free than caged. I hope.*

Callimar gave him a hood to put over his head, like hers, and Corwin did so. Then she beckoned to him again and he followed. They went down the long corridor of cells, through a door, into another corridor. But the cells along this wall were different. They had hatch seals instead of grates. Callimar went to one and turned the wheel to open it. Nia was lying inside, pale and not moving.

Nia became vaguely aware of shapes moving around her. "No, Ma'el. I won't join you," she muttered. "No, Joab. Get out of my mind." But the pain didn't come, as it had before. There was no torment wracking her body. Only a tapping on her cheek. Someone was saying her name over and over again. It was like the cry of that strange bird, Nag, that had followed Corwin around.

The water surged beside her. Her gills fluttered: she could feel them moving. Faces wavered before her. One looked like Corwin. The other looked like . . . Callimar? *No, no, this must be an illusion—I'm being tricked again.* Nia tried to push them away.

"Nia!"

This time the voice sounded a lot like Callimar. Again the water flowed around her and suddenly Nia jolted fully awake. She opened her eyes wide and saw that it was indeed Callimar, fanning the water in Nia's cell with her tail.

"Calli—"

Her friend's hand clamped over her mouth. "Shhh! We've got to get you out of here." Arms reached in to drag Nia out.

To Nia's relief, she saw now that the other face did indeed belong to Corwin. Nia collapsed against him, holding onto him tightly. He held her back, his arms strong and reassuring.

"Are you all right, Nia?"

"Better now," Nia said, nuzzling against him.

"This isn't the place for that," Callimar hissed. "We've got to keep moving." Callimar put a white hood over Nia's head.

Nia recovered her wits at last. "The sword. We've got to get the sword, Callimar. In the storage room south of Ma'el's control room."

"Whatever you say," Callimar said, her face grim. "This way."

Nia followed her former friend out to the end of the corridor of cells. "Why are you helping us?" she asked, confused. Then a new, frightening thought struck her. "Or are you just leading us to something worse?"

"No, I wouldn't—I'm so sorry," Callimar said, her voice full of pain. "Nia, I couldn't sleep after you went away. I kept worrying about you. I hated keeping my mouth shut whenever my family said they hoped you'd been caught. And then I heard that you *were* caught, and I just felt sick. You were right, Nia. This deal with Ma'el is making us just as evil as he is. I couldn't stand it any longer. It was easy for me to get work here so I could help you. If you can defeat Ma'el, I'll help in any way I can."

"Thank you, Callimar. That means a lot," Nia said, feeling warm inside for the first time since she'd been here.

Callimar led them back to the storage room. They saw no other servants along the way.

"Where is everyone?" Nia asked.

"There are uprisings all over Atlantis. Word that the last Avatar has returned is spreading and it's rallying everyone's hopes. Ma'el has his hands full right now. At least, I hope he does." Callimar turned the scallop-shaped handle and opened the storage room door.

Nia swam in, closely followed by Corwin. This time she didn't hesitate but swam straight to the pile of swords. Eikis Calli Werr lay there, its gleaming blade unmistakable among the other ordinary swords. Nia reached for Eikis Calli Werr and began to draw it out of the pile. The silvery blade glimmered, answering the energy in Nia's hand.

"It is beautiful," Callimar said. "I'd seen it carried in parades, but never up close."

"If we're lucky," Nia said, "it'll save us all." She closed her hands over the hilt, over the oculus. *Awaken*, she thought with every ounce of her concentration.

The writing etched into the blade began to glow with blue light. She felt the sword pull her arms up, to hold it upraised. Then, to her astonishment, it pulled itself out of her hands. The sword drifted over to Corwin, and offered itself, hilt first, to him.

"What's going on?" Corwin asked.

"I don't know," Nia said, feeling oddly jealous. "It was originally made to be carried by a land-dweller. Maybe it's chosen you."

Corwin cautiously grasped the hilt. His eyes shut and

he tilted his head back. Lightning bolts of green energy traveled from the hilt up his arm.

"What's happening, Corwin?"

"It . . . it hasn't chosen me, but I can carry it for a while. The oculus . . . isn't just one mind. It has absorbed, through the unis, a bit of every Farworlder king that ever lived. That's why it's so powerful. That's what Ma'el doesn't know. Ma'el only knows he's missing power and he doesn't know why. He thought that power would come from us, and that's why he captured us."

"So that's what they were trying to pull out of my mind," Nia murmured. "And since I couldn't tell them . . ." She turned to Callimar. "We've got to find our Farworlder, Gobaith, now!"

"Joab has him," Corwin grunted, still under the influence of the sword. "Joab is . . . torturing him. Trying to learn what he knows."

"But where?" Nia demanded.

"Joab's tank is this way," Callimar said. She led them back along the corridor toward Ma'el's control chamber but took a left turn. Farther down this new corridor was another round hatch door, but with a difference. Instead of a wheel in the center, this door had a latch in the shape of a Farworlder, surrounded by a circle of symbols. Nia didn't know the meaning of the symbols, but she knew what they were. This was the language of the Farworlders themselves, used before they ever founded Atlantis, before they'd come to Earth.

"Which one do I point the latch at?" Nia asked Callimar.

"I don't know. I've never opened this door. It's forbidden."

"I think I can find out," Corwin said. He pointed the sword at the lock and stared at it for a long time.

"Well?" Nia was growing impatient. She could feel a connection to Gobaith again. He was on the other side of the door. And he was in great, great pain.

"I think . . . this one, this one, then this one." Corwin pointed the tip of the sword to the left side of the circle, the right and then straight down.

Nia tried it . . . left, right and down. She pulled on the door. It didn't budge.

"No," Corwin corrected her. "Sorry, it should have been this one second." He pointed to a different symbol on the right side.

Nia sighed and tried again. She pointed the head of the Farworlder-shaped latch to the left, then to the new symbol on the right, then down. The door clicked.

Nia and Callimar hauled on the door to open it, and Nia swam right in. But when she saw what was before her, she nearly blacked out. It was a sight more horrifying that anything she'd ever seen.

The floor was made of polished metal, and Gobaith was stretched out upon it, each of his tentacles tied to a metal spike. On the head of each spike was carved a symbol much like the ones on the door. Joab floated over Gobaith, sending bolts of energy to different combinations of the spikes. Every time a green bolt of light went from Joab's tentacles to the spikes, Gobaith shuddered in pain. Nia could feel an echoing ache, even though her body was very different from the Farworlder's.

"Joab! Stop this at once!" Nia commanded. She didn't have much power in her, but she summoned what energy she had into her right hand and sent a cracking bolt of white light into Joab's hide. *At least it may get his attention*.

Joab turned to glare at her, and Nia could feel the hate and anger flowing off him. His head-mantle flared and he billowed out the skirt of skin between his tentacles, making him seem twice as large in size.

Nia refused to be intimidated. "Set Gobaith free. Now."

With a roar that Nia hadn't known Farworlders could make, Joab turned his mouth-beak toward her and splayed all his tentacles wide. Jetting water out of his siphons, he rushed at her, wrapping his tentacles around her. Nia could feel his sharp beak stabbing into her gut—

But Corwin was right on top of Joab, stabbing down through the Farworlder's head-mantle with the sword. Purple blood gushed out through the wound. The tentacles surrounding Nia shuddered and then went slack. Joab's body fell away from her and down to the floor.

Corwin jerked the blade out of Joab's head. "All I had to do was point . . . the sword knew where to go."

Corwin was right—the sword had precisely aimed itself to cut into and destroy Joab's oculus. Nia realized that she was waiting for something, but she didn't know what it was. And then it came to her. "When a king dies, his Avatar dies also."

From somewhere in the stronghold came a horrible scream.

Chapter Ten

"Is it possible?" Corwin asked as the sound of the scream trailed off through the water. "Did we kill them both at once?"

"We'd better make sure," Nia said. "But first, let's untie Gobaith."

"Gladly." Corwin went to the poor Farworlder splayed out on the floor and slashed at the bonds that held him. Corwin was amazed at the precise aim of Eikis Calli Werr, how the sword made the blood sing in his arms. He could even feel the wisdom of the Farworlder ancestors emanating from the hilt. It wasn't like his connection to Gobaith, direct and personal. It was distant magnificence, like sunlight streaming through towering clouds, a glimpse of the Divine Infinite. Corwin also knew that these ancestors had measured and weighed him and found him unworthy. The sword wasn't for him, although they'd let him bear it for a time.

The last bond was cut and Corwin gathered up the

limp Gobaith in his arms. "How are you, little fellow? Should we heal you now?"

Weakly, Gobaith sent, *I will recover. But we may be too late.*

"Too late? But Joab is dead, and Ma'el can't be far behind him."

Hmmm. I wonder. Their bond was no longer a natural one.

"Why don't you go look for Ma'el's body," Nia suggested. "I'll stay here and heal Gobaith."

Corwin handed Gobaith to Nia and swam out the door. Heading down the corridor, he imagined what he might find. He pictured Ma'el lying in a moaning heap on the floor of his control room, begging for mercy, offering to teach him the wisdom of the ages if his life were spared. Corwin would raise the sword and say . . . and say . . .

Corwin paused in front of the hatch to Ma'el's control room.

I should think of something perfect to say, he thought. After all, this was certainly a rare moment. *Maybe there's some important question I should demand an answer to, something only Ma'el would know that would help us restore Atlantis. Maybe—*

The hatch burst open and Ma'el rushed out of the room with a horrific, hate-filled roar. "You stupid, insignificant fool! What have you done?" Small rivulets of blood flowed out from beneath Ma'el's armor. He shouted angry, incomprehensible words, and the water around them turned red. Ma'el was assembling the kraken right before Corwin's eyes.

Corwin slashed with the sword—so slow in the water—at the serpent's neck. But Eikis Calli Werr cut true and the kraken's head fell away . . . only to be replaced by a new one growing out of the stump. Corwin swam around the kraken to get at Ma'el. But just as Corwin got near the evil mermyd, the kraken would swim between them, maw wide open, ready to swallow him.

Ma'el's right, I am an idiot! Again Corwin slashed with the sword and sliced off the scarlet snake's head, and again the head grew anew. Again Corwin swam past it. But each time, Ma'el was getting a little farther ahead. Corwin swam around a bend in the corridor to find it blocked by a seething, roiling mass of red serpent. But there was no head. Corwin didn't know where to cut. At last, he began slashing at every coil and bend of serpent that he saw. He cut himself a bloody doorway through the mass of kraken coils and, keeping his gills shut, swam through.

Suddenly he was hit by a wall of intensely cold, superdense water, rushing at him. Corwin was pushed back and back, unable to swim against it. A strange, repetitive wail sounded through the corridor.

Out of the corner of his eye, Corwin saw Nia pull herself along the brass piping and push down on a lever. There was a loud rumble and a hiss, and the wall of cold water slowly dissipated before him.

Corwin could swim now, but it was clear that Ma'el was gone. "What happened?"

"Ma'el went out through the filtration tube," Nia said. "But he didn't bother to close the door behind him, so the water under greater pressure flowed in from the outside. It could have crushed the city if it had filled the dome."

"So he's out in the wide sea," Corwin said. "How are we going to find him?"

You don't need to chase him, Gobaith sent. *We already know where he's going.*

Corwin turned. Callimar was floating in the passageway, holding Gobaith in her arms. She looked a bit frightened and in awe of the Farworlder.

"We do?" Corwin asked.

Ma'el knows now about the centers of power. He found the map you left in the Archives. Joab learned from me what they are. They learned from Nia about the buried shrine that you and she found. Joab isn't really necessary to Ma'el anymore, with all the oculae Ma'el's absorbed. That's why he's still alive, with Joab dead. If Ma'el can find a center of power and use it, he'll be just as powerful without Joab, if not more so. Ma'el is headed for the center of power in your land, Corwin. It's the only one left that works, although with its power Ma'el might be able to restore the rest of them throughout the world. If he succeeds, there will be no stopping him, even with the sword.

"Then we have to go back to Wales, right now!" Corwin was startled by the silence that greeted his words. "Well? Don't we?"

Nia frowned. "Yes, I guess so. It's just . . . things are so unsettled here. I hate to leave my home like this when so much rebuilding needs to be done."

"Didn't you hear Gobaith? If Ma'el uses the center of power, there won't be any point in rebuilding. He'll just conquer it all again!"

"Of course. You're right." Nia crossed her arms over her chest and gazed down at the floor. "It's just—well, healing Gobaith took a lot out of me."

"Do you feel well enough to swim out to the transfer point?"

There's no need for that, Gobaith sent.

"What?"

Joab's quarters have the necessary equipment and engines to be a transfer point. He and Ma'el had been constructing it for weeks. Joab threatened to send me to all sorts of horrible places.

"Then why didn't Ma'el make his escape that way?"

Because only a Farworlder can operate it, and Joab is dead.

With one tentacle, Gobaith tapped Callimar's shoulder and pointed back the way they had come. Callimar turned and swam back down the corridor.

Corwin followed her, one hand holding Eikis Calli Werr, the other on Nia's shoulder. "Are you all right?" he asked her softly.

"Yes—no." Nia put her arm through Corwin's. "I'm just afraid of leaving and not coming back again. Atlantis seems so precious now that I'm here."

"But that's always been a risk, hasn't it?"

"Yes, of course, but . . . it's hard to explain."

"All right." Corwin decided he was just going to have to live with that. But there was one thing he needed to say. "When I was taken away by Joab, I thought I heard you think something at me."

"Oh?"

"Something . . . nice."

"Really?"

"Something I wouldn't mind hearing again."

"Yes?"

"You're going to make me ask, aren't you?" Corwin paused and waited until Callimar and Gobaith were well ahead. "Did you mean it when you said . . . you said . . ."

"That I love you?" Nia turned, smiled and kissed him full on the lips. This wasn't a kiss for breathing, but it certainly left Corwin breathless. For a few precious moments, she opened her mind and heart to him, and he knew that it was true.

Haste would be a good idea, Gobaith sent.

Nia pulled back and for once Corwin had less than friendly thoughts toward the young Farworlder.

Yes, yes, I know, Gobaith sent. *I don't mean to ruin your happiness, but Ma'el will ruin it for good if he isn't stopped.*

"It's so much more annoying when he's right," Corwin muttered.

"Isn't it though?" Nia agreed.

Reluctantly, they turned and followed Callimar and Gobaith back to Joab's lair.

Nia and Corwin swam in, watching as Gobaith flitted around the room, turning dials to point at different symbols and sliding back panels to reveal rows of glowing crystals in tidy array. *They did an amazing job*, Gobaith sent. *This will be much easier to work than the old transfer point we used to get here.*

"But when did you learn how to work it?" Nia asked.

It's difficult to keep one mind closed if two minds are joined. While Joab was absorbing my knowledge, I was also absorbing his. It didn't concern him, since he didn't expect me to get free.

Gobaith pulled another lever, and a circular panel in the floor slid back.

Nia went to Callimar and took her hands. "We have to go after Ma'el. But I'm worried about our people."

"Don't worry, Nia," Callimar reassured her. "I will make sure my family does everything we can to set things back in order."

"What I'm afraid of," Nia began, "is trading one tyrant for another. Your family knows what it's like to rule now."

Callimar's eyes flashed. "And we know what tyrants are like. We are Atlanteans, not land-dwellers. We will see that Atlantis stays well cared for until the Avatar . . . Avatars return."

Nia hoped Callimar meant it. Her words seemed sincere, at least. "Thank you, Callimar. We're counting on you."

"I know. Good luck, Nia." Callimar hugged her. She

turned to Corwin and said, "For the glowing sea-snails!"

"What?" Corwin shook his head in bafflement.

Callimar grinned. "That's the new rallying cry among the Atlantean rebels, didn't you know? I heard it came from you. What does it mean, anyway?"

"Oh. Right. Well, um, it's . . . metaphorical. Deep meaning, shaded in layers of—"

"Come *on*, Corwin."

Nia sighed and went to the glowing spot on the floor. Corwin waved to Callimar and went to stand beside Nia. Gobaith was by the controls, cradling the sword in his tentacles. Nia reached out mentally and discovered that Gobaith was communing with the oculus in the hilt. Gobaith seemed to be in a state of momentary bliss.

"Speaking to his ancestors," Corwin said, nodding at the Farworlder. "I'll be lucky to get the sword back from him."

"I wonder what he's learning."

"As much as possible about how to get us where we're going, I hope."

Nia just hoped he wasn't learning anything she didn't want to know. She couldn't tell Corwin the reason that she was so reluctant to go—while she'd been healing Gobaith, Nia had had . . . not so much a vision but an impression, a feeling. A feeling she wasn't going to see

Atlantis again, not anytime soon. The unis could only show the near future, of course. Further events were too much in flux to be clear or certain. But still . . .

Gobaith finished his immersion in the souls of his ancestors and brought the sword back to Corwin. *What a wonderful, wonderful thing. I wish I could carry it always. But it isn't for me.*

"You can hold it all you like," Corwin said, "as long as you let me have it back when it's time to fight Ma'el."

No, Gobaith sent. *There's something I have to tell you. I'm not coming with you.*

"WHAT?" Nia and Corwin exclaimed at the same time.

While I was being interrogated by Joab, I learned that not all of the infant Farworlders were killed. Ma'el intends to breed and raise them, so that he will always have fresh oculae to harvest. I have to find them and protect them. I can't desert them—if they aren't given proper nurturing, they could be very dangerous, to the mermyds as well as themselves.

Nia and Corwin exchanged a horrified glance. "But what if we need your magic and your energy?" Nia protested.

You have the sword now. It will give you more than I could. And I can always offer advice, even from far away. Please understand, and don't be upset. There's much good I can do here. I will help Callimar rebuild Atlantis, too.

"We'll miss you, little squid," Corwin said.

And I will miss you, Gobaith sent. *Now prepare yourselves. I suggest you both hold onto the sword.*

Nia and Corwin stepped close together. Each grasped hold of the hilt of Eikis Calli Werr, and put the other hand around each other's waist. Gobaith went to the control panel with its symbols and dials and crystals. Nia closed her eyes, feeling strangely helpless. If fate had determined that she and Corwin were going to be defeated, what was the point?

But she reminded herself that the prophecy of the High Council about her had been misinterpreted. Maybe she was misinterpreting this vision from the unis, too. As Corwin rested his forehead against the top of her head, Nia felt the energy from the oculus in the sword hilt flow over her. She could almost hear the voices of the Farworlder ancestors whispering in her mind. She wanted to ask them, *Will I die?* But they weren't interested in her question. Instead, they probed her mind for images of Corwin's land, of places she remembered the best. They were preparing to bend the unis, to send Nia and Corwin where they had to go.

Good-bye! Good luck! Gobaith pulled down on a lever and again, Nia felt the gut-wrenching sensation of the world falling away from them, of being free of the pull of the Earth, free of water, free of air, free of the need to breathe or to have a heartbeat.

Corwin and Nia spun around and the sword flipped up, out from between them, to point over their heads. Nia and Corwin held each other closer as the sword pulled them swiftly through the folded unis. Nia kept her eyes shut, not wanting to see the strange geometrices of this other side of the universe. Probably even the wisest instructors who had ever served at the Academy had no names for what they were passing through. Selfishly, Nia realized she wished she could just stay here, suspended in time and space, with no more struggle, no more pain, holding onto Corwin forever.

With a shock, a splash and a crack of thunder, they fell into cold water. Saltwater. Nia's feet struck sand and she let go of Corwin and the sword. To her surprise, her head popped above the surface. Corwin surfaced a moment later, still holding the sword. Wiping the water from her eyes, Nia glanced around. They were in Carmarthen Bay.

Chapter Eleven

"Well aimed, Gobaith," Corwin murmured as he wiped the water from his eyes. The sun was lowering in the sky to the west. The leaves on the trees were tinged with gold in anticipation of autumn. Corwin realized how strange it had been to be in a world where he didn't know the time of day, or the season of the year, at a glance. "We arrived more swiftly and smoothly than the first time. I'll give Ma'el credit for that: he builds a better people-sender."

"If only he'd used his skills to help Atlantis instead of destroy it," Nia commented. She began to walk out of the water, slogging through the shallows as though she felt very heavy.

"I guess you're not too happy about being back in this big dry room I call home," Corwin said. For the first time, he realized that he really did think of Britannia as his home. *Is it just that it feels good to be somewhere familiar?* he wondered. *Or am I really tied to this land in my soul?*

And what does that mean for my future with Nia?

Corwin waded out of the ocean and up onto the rocky strand. "The question now," he said, "is where, exactly, do we find Ma'el?"

"At the *shrine*," Nia replied. "The center of power."

"Mmm-hmm. And do you happen to remember where that is?"

Nia frowned. "Between here and Castle Carmarthen?"

"Yes, but that covers a lot of ground."

"Somewhere past that foggy pond?"

"Right." Corwin sighed. "And where's the foggy pond?"

"It's . . . I thought *you* knew where it was!"

"Well it's not like we thought it was important at the time, did we? We just stumbled across it while we had other places to go."

Nia sat down on a rock. "Of course. Why did I expect this to be easy?"

Corwin sat down beside her. "Look, the good news is, if we don't know where it is, Ma'el doesn't either, since he got the information about it from *your* mind."

"And the map in the Archives."

"The map wasn't very specific . . . it just showed this big dot that could be anywhere within a hundred miles of here."

"I hope you're right," Nia said.

"I know I'm right," Corwin said, with a little more confidence than he felt. "Maybe this magic sword can point the way." Corwin held it up and pointed it toward the forest-crested cliffs. "Oooo Eikis Calli Werr, oh mighty magic sword, point the way to the Atlantean center of power," he intoned.

Nia rolled her eyes.

The sword wavered a bit and then the point fell back into the water, narrowly missing Corwin's foot. "Hey!"

"I don't think the Farworlder ancestors want to be toyed with," Nia said. "Besides, maybe if the center isn't active, there's nothing for the sword to sense."

"So we won't be able to know how to find it until Ma'el is already there and using it?" Corwin looked at the sword. "Big help *you* are."

"The sword wasn't made to do *everything*," Nia said. "It was only supposed to help bring peace."

Corwin nodded, noting that the sun was continuing to lower. "Ma'el might send the kraken again to slow us down," he said. "We need to find shelter somewhere and figure this all out."

"Where should we go?" Nia asked.

An hour later, as the sun was setting, Corwin, with Nia leaning on his shoulder, was knocking on the rotting door of Henwyneb's cottage. He heard a raucous cry within. "Rawk-rawk-rawk-rawk!"

"No . . . it couldn't be . . . "

The door creaked open. The wrinkled, sightless face of old Henwyneb the button-maker, appeared in the doorway. "Who is it?"

"It's Corwin, the fellow who used to sell you shells and nearly got you in trouble with royalty."

"Corwin! So that's your name. Come in, come in!"

"And was that noise I heard——"

A black, feathered projectile zoomed past his head and arrowed for the trees beyond, lightly raking his face with its talons as it passed.

"Nice to see you again too, Nag!" Corwin called, rubbing his cheek.

"Oh, ignore him," Henwyneb said. "He's as rude as any cat. Caws to be let in, caws to be let out. When he first called at my door, I thought you were done for, so I let him in out of kindness. Now he's made himself at home and made a mess of it. Come in, come in."

Nia laughed. "It's good to see some things don't change."

Henwyneb gasped again. "Is this the mermaid lady of Atlantis returning as well?"

"It is," Corwin said. "And I've told her such wondrous

things about your cooking that she decided she has to sample it."

"I'm afraid you must prepare yourself for disappointment, my lady, but you're welcome to try it." Henwyneb stepped back from the door and Corwin and Nia walked in.

The smell of the fish soup on the hearth did make Corwin's stomach growl. He politely helped Nia to one of the two wooden stools and then sat on the rush-strewn floor. He felt instantly at home and at peace and wondered how some people's houses could seem so inviting, no matter how well or poorly furnished.

Henwyneb ladled out the soup in bowls and gave them to Corwin and Nia. "Now tell me all your adventures since I last saw you."

"There's a lot to tell and we don't have much time." Still, Corwin related an abbreviated version of everything that had happened after they'd last left Henwyneb's home.

"There were rumors," Henwyneb said when Corwin finished, "that King Vortigern was chased away by a red dragon that appeared in his cellars. These rumors included the detail that a certain ward of a certain charlatan named Fenwyck had prophesied that very thing. I don't suppose you'd know anything more about that?"

"Well," Corwin said. "For one thing, it was a kraken, not

a dragon, and that wasn't quite the vision I'd had and . . . oh, this is getting too complicated. Let's just say we found what we wanted and returned to Atlantis to try to destroy the evil king Ma'el, who had terrorized Nia's people. We didn't quite succeed. And we have reason to think Ma'el has come back here to use that ruined shrine—it's called a center of power by Nia's people—to gain final control over the world. We have to stop him before he does."

"Ah," Henwyneb said. "I think I know what you're describing. Even the druids won't go near that place. They say its power is too great, too potentially dangerous—it's a magic of a world beyond our world."

"That sounds like our shrine," Corwin said, with an excited glance at Nia. "But we don't know if we can find it again. We weren't really paying attention the first time we stumbled across it. Is there any way you could give us a better idea of where it is exactly?"

"Well, I could lead you there myself, if I had my sight," Henwyneb said. "I used to play near those ruins as a boy. I even slipped inside once and saw marvelous wall carvings . . . couldn't make heads or tails of them, though. I was pretty frightened, so I made sure I knew where it was in order to avoid ending up there again."

"You said you could lead us if you had your sight," Nia

said. "And I did promise you that if I returned, I would use my healing powers to give it back to you. Would you still like that?"

Henwyneb's jaw dropped. "Dear lady," he breathed, "you don't know what I would give for such a gift."

"You don't need to give us anything," Corwin said. "Just show us the way to the shrine."

"Gladly, gladly," Henwyneb agreed. "Whenever you're ready to begin, my lady."

Nia stood and went to Henwyneb, placing her hands over his eyes. Corwin could feel her summon the energy from both him and Gobaith. It was amazing how the connection with Gobaith remained strong, even though they were so many miles apart. A glow radiated from Nia's hands, flowing over the old man's face and down over his chest, arms and legs. Henwyneb's eyes soon echoed the glow until it seemed as though he was lit from within. His face was upturned in a rapturous smile. Corwin remembered how wonderful the healing had felt when he and Nia had performed the Naming with Gobaith, and he smiled too.

Nia stepped back, reeling a little. Corwin stood and put his arm around her shoulders to steady her.

Henwyneb sighed . . . and opened his eyes. They were now a clear light blue. Henwyneb stood straighter. He gazed around the room, smiling. "I never knew how wondrous sight is," he said softly, "until I lost it. Now that I have it again, I see myself surrounded by miracles." His gaze finally fell on Nia. "The greatest of which is you, good lady." He bowed to her. "With all my heart, I thank you."

Nia bowed back. "You're very welcome, good Henwyneb."

"We don't expect you to guide us in the dark," Corwin said. "So if it's okay for us to stay the night here, we can be on our way at dawn."

"You're as welcome here as if you were family," Henwyneb replied. "Although, given the nature of many people's families, perhaps more so."

So Henwyneb set out straw mats on the floor for Corwin and Nia to sleep on and gave them worn, threadbare blankets to sleep under.

There came a raucous cawing and banging at the door.

"Oh very well, you demanding creature." Henwyneb went to the door and opened it.

Nag flew in, then flew around the room cawing and cawing. He finally landed at Corwin's feet and glared up at him. "Well, what do you want *me* to do?" Corwin asked.

Nag stretched one wing, as if pointing it toward the door. "AWK!"

Corwin sighed and made a show of looking out the

door. It was utterly black outside, the light from the fire inside the hovel only revealing a little of Henwyneb's herb garden. Corwin stuck his head back in and shut the door. "There's nothing to see out there, Nag. And we can't do any good blundering about in the dark. You might as well calm yourself and stay in for the night."

Nag ruffled his feathers and jumped up to the mantle above the hearth. There was a wooden carving of the head of a Roman goddess wearing a helmet sitting on the mantle. The raven hopped onto it and perched there, glaring at everyone.

"A good choice," Henwyneb said. "That's Minerva, goddess of wisdom. Perhaps she can deliver some to your tiny brain. In the meantime, good night. Good night to you all."

Nia settled on her mat in the center of the room. Henwyneb took to his pallet. Corwin stretched out on his back beside the hearth, letting the heat from the lowering fire warm and soothe him. To his surprise, as he was drifting off, Corwin felt something moving in the crook of his arm. Nag had hopped next to him and nestled there, tucking his beak under his wing. Corwin idly scratched the bird on the back between the wings, and then he drifted off to sleep.

Corwin's slumber wasn't peaceful, however. He dreamed that Nag was pecking at his arm and chest, trying to rouse him, cawing loudly in his face. But Corwin couldn't move, other than to open his eyes and turn his head. A black cloud was drifting in through the cracks around the door to the hovel. The cloud drifted near the ceiling, seeking something.

Suddenly the black cloud plunged down, pouring over Corwin, enveloping him in cold darkness. Memories of the evening's conversation with Henwyneb replayed themselves. Corwin remembered when Gobaith had delved into his memories, and Corwin called out to the Farworlder, "Gobaith? Gobaith, are you there?" But there was no response.

The black cloud lifted from Corwin and rose up to the ceiling. Again it plunged down, this time onto Nia. She struggled and moaned a little as it enveloped her. Corwin tried to struggle, too, but he was still completely unable to move.

After a few moments, the cloud lifted from her and this time went directly to Henwyneb. The cloud flowed over the old man who cried out once from the enveloping darkness. Then the cloud lifted for the final time and flowed back out under the hovel door. Corwin fell into a heavy, dreamless sleep.

Chapter Twelve

Nia felt someone shake her shoulder.

"Nia! Nia! Are you okay?"

Her eyelids felt rough and sandy as she opened them. Corwin was bending over her, his eyes wide with terror.

"Corwin? What's wrong?" Nia slowly sat up. It was like trying to swim through mud.

"I had a bad dream," Corwin said. "Only I'm beginning to think it wasn't a dream. Did you dream?"

Nia squinted as she tried to remember. "Yes, I did," she said finally. "I was swimming in very dark water. Someone called out to me. I thought it was the ancestors in the sword, but it was just someone disguised as the ancestors. They were probing my mind, trying to find something. The real Farworlder ancestors were protecting me, though. After a while, I was out of the dark water. That's all, I think."

"Someone tried to replay my memories in my dream," Corwin said. "Help me wake up Henwyneb."

Nia went with him to Henwyneb's bedside. The old man was still asleep, but frowning as if struggling with inner demons.

"Henwyneb!" Corwin shook his shoulder, too.

"Uhhh!" The old man clumsily tried to push Corwin away.

Nia placed her hands on either side of his head and tried to send cleansing energy into his mind. "Henwyneb, please wake up."

With a jolt and a jerk, Henwyneb opened his eyes. "Oh my, oh my," he breathed.

"Did you have nightmares too?" Nia asked.

"It was much worse than a nightmare," Henwyneb said, his face still full of fear. "A dark spirit appeared to me and demanded to know where the center of power was in the woods. When I wouldn't tell him, he flowed into my mind and I couldn't hide a single thought from him. This spirit dredged from me every memory of where the ancient shrine is hidden."

Nia and Corwin looked at each other. "Ma'el!" they said in unison.

"Then we've lost," Corwin said. "He must be there by now."

"It might take him a while to learn how to use the

shrine," Nia pointed out. "Henwyneb, please, can you lead us there quickly?"

"As quick as this old body can manage, my lady," Henwyneb said, swinging his feet over the cot and standing. "Which is much quicker than it once was, thanks to your healing powers."

Nia picked up Eikis Calli Werr from the mat. It hummed in her hands, as if sensing the battle yet to come. Or maybe it was resonating with whatever power was being conjured in the shrine.

Henwyneb pulled down a gnarled walking stick from a hook on the wall. He went to the door and held it open as Nia and Corwin stepped out into the morning.

A mist was rising from the ground, getting thicker in the air.

"This isn't normal weather for this time of year," Corwin muttered.

"No, but it won't matter," Henwyneb said. "As a formerly blind man, a little mist isn't a problem for me. Come along."

Nia and Corwin hurried after Henwyneb. The old man ducked in and out of the trees of the woods as if he knew where every bush and tree root was hidden. Nia stumbled now and then, especially since she had to get used to walking on dry land all over again. Air just couldn't hold a person up as well as water. But Eikis Calli Werr swung in her hand and planted its point just where it would brace her from falling. Corwin stumbled too sometimes, but he tried to alter his gait to hide it, saying, "I meant to do that."

It was a strange journey, with no sense of time or location. Nia felt as disoriented as she had during the passage through the folded unis. All around them, the forest was silent, except for their footsteps crashing through the underbrush. That and one other noise.

Somewhere along the way, they'd been joined by Nag, Corwin's bedeviling bird, who was making quiet, querulous "awk? awk?" sounds. The raven seemed nearly as smart as Ki-ki, but not nearly as good-natured. Still, Nia sensed that the bird was concerned for their welfare, as it glided from branch to branch, following them.

Nia smelled water on the air and stopped.

"What is it?" Corwin asked.

"The pond. The one I swam in. It's nearby, isn't it?"

"Probably," Corwin said. He frowned. "Why?"

"Nothing, I just . . . *sense* it." The pond had been strangely soothing last time she was there, and part of her wished she could stop and linger again for a while. But saving the world was a bit more important than a few moments of comfort.

"Let's push on," Corwin said. "You don't have time for a swim." Corwin sounded unusually gruff, and Nia remembered that he'd been afraid of the pond. She still didn't know why. *I'll ask Corwin about the pond again when all this is over.*

Suddenly Nia ran right into Henwyneb's back, not noticing that he had stopped.

"Ohhhh!" Henwyneb's arms pinwheeled and he fell forward, sliding down the hole that Nia and Corwin had found weeks before. Unable to find her own balance, Nia fell also. Eikis Calli Werr kept her from falling on her face, but she turned and slid on her bottom down a ramp of gravel to a marble floor below.

Behind them, Corwin, for once the image of gracefulness, stayed on his two feet as he skittered down the chute.

"Ow, that hole wasn't so large the last time I was here," Henwyneb said, putting a hand to his back.

Nia got up and helped him stand, sending a little healing energy into his back.

"It's bigger than it was when we came by here, too," Corwin observed. "And better lit."

Nia let her eyes adjust to the darkness and saw that it wasn't actually that dark. A dim glow that grew brighter to the east ahead of them illuminated the circular entry chamber.

Carvings covered the walls, showing scenes of life from Atlantis and mermyds greeting and interacting with land-dwellers. One panel showed the Farworlders coming in their sky-ship from the stars and entering the ocean to found their city and create the race of mermyds.

"This was built in a more peaceful time," Nia murmured. "The Farworlders clearly expected their friendship with land-dwellers to last."

"We have to keep going," Corwin said, his hand on her shoulder.

Nia could feel his hand shaking slightly, and she rested her hand on his. "We'll get through this. We have to."

A low growl and roar echoed out to them from somewhere deep within the shrine ahead.

"Right. Let's go in before the little bit of courage I have disappears," Corwin said. "May I carry the sword?"

Nia smiled and handed him Eikis Calli Werr, hilt first. Corwin let his hand linger over Nia's for a moment before he took the sword from her.

"Rawk-rawk-rawk!" Nag cried from behind them.

"Shhhhhhh!" all three turned to shush the bird.

"Henwyneb, could you shoo the bird out?" Corwin asked. "He's going to give us away."

"Gladly. Go on, you nasty beast." Henwyneb fluttered his hands at Nag, to no effect.

"Shoo."

"Rawk."

"Shoo!"

"Rawk!"

"SHOO!"

"RAWK!"

Finally, Henwyneb scooped Nag up in his arms and—holding tightly onto the scratching, biting bird—he walked back toward the entry. "Hurry on, you two. I'll take care of Master Loudmouth here."

"Thank you, Henwyneb," Nia said.

"Though it's probably too late," Corwin said.

They both headed to the doorway across the broad, circular room. There was a stairway leading down. The eerie light was brighter toward the bottom. A low moaning, as if someone was in tortuous pain, drifted up to them. Nia's skin crawled at the sound.

"You'd better let me go first," Corwin said.

"Why?"

"Because I have the sword. And that means that someone coming our way would meet the pointy end of the sword first."

"That makes sense," Nia agreed with a small smile.

Corwin placed his back against the wall of the stairwell and sidled down it sideways, sword held at the ready. Nia had always felt a little strange about Corwin's past as a thief, but she could see now that it had given him some useful skills.

Corwin stopped at the bottom of the stairs and peered out from the lower archway. Apparently he didn't see anything, because he began to step out . . . and pulled his foot immediately back, as the flagstone just beyond the bottom step dropped away.

Corwin motioned for Nia to stay utterly still, and he did too for several long heartbeats. Heavy silence filled the shrine. Then a deep gong sounded somewhere in the distance.

"That does it," Corwin said. "We've announced ourselves as surely as a bell on a door."

"We might as well keep going, then," Nia suggested.

Corwin nodded once, then studied the floor of the chamber ahead. It was made up entirely of square-cut flagstones, just like the one that had dropped away under Corwin's foot.

"Let me guess," Corwin said. "There's some pattern, significant to your people, that's safe to walk, but anyone else will fall through the floor into a pit where horrible, devouring creatures are waiting. So, Nia, what pattern should we walk?"

Nia concentrated hard. She thought, as she gazed at the flagstones, that she could make out a sort of map of Atlantis. It was again a circular chamber, and the largest stone, white marble with some gold inlay, was at the center. Any greedy land-dweller would of course have headed for the gold. But someone from Atlantis would know. . . .

"The fastest way around Atlantis is in the rim current. We used to swim it as children, even though our parents told us we couldn't."

"What does that have to do with here?" Corwin asked.

"You taught me about maps, Corwin, remember? This floor is a rough map of Atlantis." Nia gazed along the walls. A circle of blue-tinted stones encircled the room at the edge.

"So let's try to run the rim current here." Nia positioned herself at the rightmost edge of the bottom-most step. Swinging her right leg out over the hole left where the flagstone had dropped, Nia placed her right foot on the first blue flagstone of the outer circle. Slowly, she put her weight on it. It held. "I'm right, Corwin!"

Corwin quickly came over to her side of the stairway and slid over onto the same stone. It slowly began to move down.

With a cry of alarm, Nia hopped onto the next stone in the circle. It, too, began to slowly descend. Nia went to the next, which fell away a little faster. She began to run around the circle, Corwin following hard on her heels. By the time she got to the opposite side of the room, she was running as fast as she could, as the stones fell away faster and faster.

At last, Nia flung herself through the far doorway and lay on the cool stone floor. Corwin was right behind her and slid beside her seconds later. They could hear stone grinding against stone as the entire outer circle fell away, down into darkness.

"Well, you were right about one thing," Corwin said. "That was the *fastest* way through."

"I'm sorry it wasn't the easiest," Nia said. "But at least we got here."

She began to get up, but Corwin grabbed her tunic and pulled her back down. "Nia, watch out!" he cried, as she fell to the floor again.

Nia was about to turn and yell at him when a heavy stone block swung out from the wall to their right and slammed into the wall to their left. Then it swung back, silently, into the wall.

Nia looked up at where the stone had struck the wall—at about head height.

"It would have crushed you," Corwin said.

"Thank you," Nia said, her heart pounding loudly in her chest.

"Maybe we should go the rest of the way on our hands and knees?" Corwin suggested.

"I think that's a good idea."

Together they crawled forward to the next archway. The chamber beyond had a high, domed ceiling and a floor of plain, polished black stone. There was nothing else in the chamber, no carvings on the circular wall.

Nia sensed something was wrong, but she couldn't quite piece together what it was.

"Hmmm, no holes in the walls or ceiling, none in the floor," Corwin observed. "Maybe the builders assumed that if you got this far, you might as well have the rest easy." He got up, poised to sprint across the room.

Nia wasn't used to having the sense of smell again. That was why it took her so long to understand what worried her. She was smelling water again. But it wasn't like the pond water. She grabbed Corwin's trouser leg. "Corwin, wait, that isn't . . ."

A flurry of black feathers passed by overhead, one wing striking Corwin on the head as it passed. "Rawk! Rawk! Rawk! Rawk!"

"Nag!" Corwin roared angrily, rubbing his temple.

As the raven flew out into the chamber, the floor rippled and roiled, swelled and undulated, turning a dark red. The head of the kraken rose up out of the floor, which Nia now realized with horror hadn't been black stone at all but absolutely still seawater. The serpent opened its gaping maw and swallowed Nag whole. As the kraken closed its jaws, Nia and Corwin could still hear Nag shrieking for a while longer as he slid down the kraken's throat. And then the sound stopped.

"Nag? Naaag!" Corwin cried out in anger and sadness.

The kraken opened its mouth again and came toward Corwin and Nia.

Corwin held up Eikis Calli Werr. As the serpent struck, he swung the sword, which neatly severed the kraken's head. The body fell back into the water, dissolving into the tiny creatures that screamed as they sank into the blackness. The only sign of Nag was a few black feathers floating on the surface.

"Stupid bird!" Corwin cried. His sorrow echoed through the high domed chamber.

Nia could see the tears forming in his eyes, and she threw her arms around Corwin. "Your raven died saving our lives, Corwin. If we'd fallen into the water unprepared, the kraken would have swallowed us before we knew what was happening."

Corwin's fist was clenched and he was shaking. "I . . . am . . . so . . . damned . . . tired of that kraken!"

Low, dark laughter echoed from the archway at the far side of the chamber.

"And I'm tired of you too, you monster!"

"Corwin, please," Nia counseled. "You'll only make Ma'el happier, knowing that he's hurt you." She gently pulled Corwin back from the edge of the pool, but not so far as to again trigger the swinging stone.

"So we're at stalemate again," Corwin growled. "Ma'el's probably re-forming the kraken even now. If we can't get past it, we can't get to him. And if he holds us off long enough, he'll have all the power he needs."

Nia gazed into the pool. What spell could destroy an enemy that just re-formed out of the creatures of the water? She wished Gobaith were with them, for guidance. She could still feel the Farworlder's presence in the back of her mind, but only his encouragement and hope. The one specific thought that came across the distance was: *What you can't defeat, learn from*. Nia remembered how Gobaith had learned much from the kraken, just by absorbing the energy from the multitude of creatures that made up the beast—and then she had it. Softly, she said, "Corwin, I know how we can destroy the kraken, once and for all."

"You do?"

Nia nodded. "We've been thinking about this wrong. Instead of simply attacking it, we should take energy from it. Drain all the magical and life energy from each little creature in it. This way, Ma'el's spell will be giving us power. As soon as Ma'el realizes he's only making us stronger, he'll dissolve the kraken at once, for good."

Corwin sucked in his breath, then nodded. "Good idea. Um, how do we do that?"

"Let me think." Nia's magical experience had mostly involved giving energy. The taking of life energy from an unwilling creature would ordinarily be repugnant to her. But this was an unnatural, monstrous creature, Nia reminded herself, and needed to be destroyed. But it was so huge, and the power contained within it, and the life energy of all the creatures that made it up, would be enormous. Nia tried to imagine containing and controlling such power, but she just couldn't.

The head of the kraken rose up again and rushed at them. Corwin sliced the serpent's head down the middle and the kraken melted again, spraying them with cold, scarlet water.

"Thought long enough?" Corwin asked. "Because the kraken can probably keep this up all day, and I don't think I can."

Nia gazed at Corwin. "It would take enormous power to drain all of the kraken, and great power to contain that energy without it destroying the one who drains it."

"All right. And?"

"And neither one of us has that much power."

Corwin looked at her. "Do you mean to tell me that we've come all this way for nothing? You said the sword would give us the power to destroy Ma'el!"

"I'm not finished, Corwin. This is like the spells we've done where one of us must give the other our power to do it. It *can* be done. But one of us must sacrifice power to the other."

"Oh. Why didn't you say so, then? So which one of us should it be?"

Nia shook her head. "You don't understand," she said softly. "The other person must give *all* of their power, *all* of their life energy."

Corwin became very still. "You mean, give up their . . . life? *Die?*"

"I—I don't know. Maybe not die . . . entirely. Maybe just sleep for a while, until the energy is given back."

"Forget it," Corwin snapped. "We're going through this

together. I didn't go to Atlantis and back just to bow out now and I couldn't bear it if you gave up your life for me."

"Corwin, it's the only way."

"Well think of another one."

The kraken came at them again, stronger this time, nearly tearing the sword from Corwin's hands before he managed to cut its neck and sever its head.

They both stood dripping with slimy red water, and Nia shivered. "It's our only chance, Corwin," she pleaded. "The kraken's getting stronger as Ma'el learns to use the center of power. Maybe . . . maybe the knowledge in Eikis Calli Werr can keep whoever gives their power from dying."

Corwin gazed at her with eyes full of fear and love. "We can't do this."

"We have to."

"But who—who will be the giver, then?"

"Why don't we let the sword decide?"

They gazed at each other for long moments before Corwin swallowed hard and said, "All right."

They placed their hands over the hilt of Eikis Calli Werr. Nia closed her eyes and opened her mind to receive the wisdom of the ancient Farworlders. *Which of us must give our power so that the other can defeat our enemy?*

The answer didn't come in words or visions. She just

knew which path in the unis led to victory. A lump formed in her throat as she remembered the fear she'd had that she would never see Atlantis again. Maybe this was why.

"No!" Corwin wailed, having also sensed the sword's decision.

Nia felt tears forming in her eyes, but she stayed brave. "Corwin, our lives are unimportant compared to the many Ma'el will destroy. And . . . and the sword will preserve me. I don't know how, but it will. I'll put my trust in the Farworlder ancestors. Listen, put me in water as soon as you can, after you've finished with Ma'el. We mermyds revive well in water." Even as she said it, she knew she was only trying to convince Corwin. She couldn't hide from the truth herself.

"Nia . . . I . . . I don't want to lose you!"

"If Ma'el succeeds, you'll lose me anyway. We would both die. And so would many others in the world, both land-dweller and mermyd."

Corwin sighed. "Yes. Yes, I know that."

"But if we do this, there's a chance we'll both be okay. And Corwin—the whole world will be saved."

Tears were leaking out of Corwin's eyes.

"Come on," Nia urged. "Let's get it done."

"One last thing." Corwin choked out. He pulled her close

and kissed her. Nia could feel his love and sorrow flowing over her like a wave that was both warm and chill, soft and sharp. Again, she wished she could stay in this moment forever, and it took all of her determination to, at last, pull away.

"Let my energy flow to you through the sword," she told him. "It will protect me by not letting you take it all. But when you fight the kraken, you can't let anything hold you back. You have to take every bit of its life force in order to kill it."

Corwin put both his hands over hers. "I . . . I understand. Oh, Nia, I don't want to do this."

"But we have to. Good luck, Corwin of Carmarthen." Nia closed her eyes and leaned against Corwin, the sword between them. She channeled her energy out of the center of her body, into the sword hilt. From there, the energy flowed into Corwin's hands. She felt her strength draining from her as if it were water flowing out from her body. She felt weakness overtake her and fear creeping in as her body cried out that it was dying. Still Nia pushed on, pouring the power through, until she was spent and the world around her faded to nothingness.

Corwin felt the power rushing in through his hands from the hilt of the sword, like cold fire coursing through his muscles. As it flowed in and in, unstoppable as a flood, he began to shake. The fire coursed into his chest, into his heart, as if he were holding wild lightning inside. He felt Nia's hands, beneath his own, loosen their grip on the hilt. As they slipped away, Corwin caught her in his right arm and gently eased her to the floor. He laid her out straight upon the flagstones and placed the sword on top of her, the tip of the hilt under her chin. Placing his hand on the flat of the blade, he whispered, "Protect her, Eikis Calli Werr, until I return." Corwin kissed Nia one last time, hoping against hope that she would be all right. Then he turned and dove into the black water.

As he'd expected, the kraken swiftly re-formed in the water around him. The serpent's eyes glowed red and the jaws opened wide.

Come and get me, Corwin thought with cold hatred.

The kraken lunged at him.

Corwin let the serpent swallow him, felt the jaws close over him, felt the seething mass of tiny creatures that made up the kraken biting into his skin. Corwin allowed them, for a moment, letting the pain feed into his anger.

And then he pulled. Having held the sword that drew the life from Nia, Corwin knew how to do it. He summoned the wild lightning of power within to draw out the life force from the kraken, as though every inch of his skin could breathe in its energy.

Corwin screamed into the water as the new energy, adding to the fires within, became too much to contain. It filled him to overflowing and he felt himself expanding outward, ready to explode. *It's too much! Too much! I can't hold it!*

Corwin realized that there would have to be a slight change of plans.

He suddenly changed the direction of the power. Instead of drinking it in, Corwin fed himself, his life force, into the millions of creatures that made up the serpent. Instead of draining the kraken, Corwin *became* the kraken.

Rising up out of the water, Corwin tested the strength of his new form. He gazed at the room with the kraken's eyes, and it was now a tiny chamber, barely large enough for him. He raced through the water with the kraken's speed. He roared with the serpent's mouth and champed with kraken jaws.

But he was still Corwin inside, and he still knew what he had to do. The Corwin/kraken circled the domed chamber twice before swimming out through the far archway and into the final chamber.

Ma'el was there, though not in any shape Corwin had seen him in before. The center of the chamber was a round raised platform on which were carved similar symbols and levers to those Corwin had seen at the transfer point. But these were arrayed in a shape that required the ten arms of a Farworlder to manipulate. And that was the form Ma'el was trying to take.

He was sprawled on the stone platform. Instead of the fish tail, Ma'el now had two tentacles sprouting from his hips. New limbs were growing from the ribs in his sides. Ma'el was spreading himself out, trying to reach for the symbols and levers in the pattern on the stone. But Corwin could see that it was painful, difficult and slow, and Ma'el hadn't completed the process yet.

Corwin roared with the kraken's scream, feeling all the little creatures that were now also Corwin screaming too. The scream echoed and reverberated through the shrine chambers, a battle cry.

Ma'el turned his now bulbous, lopsided head. "Have you at last devoured them, my friend? Well, I guess that's best. Now let me finish my work."

But the Corwin/kraken just rose higher out of the water to loom over Ma'el, who looked very small below.

Ma'el frowned. "Leave!" he ordered, but Corwin only opened his jaws wider.

At last Corwin saw on Ma'el's face what he'd been

hoping to see. Terror. The knowledge that his great plan was about to fail. Then Corwin struck, lunging down and picking up Ma'el in his jaws. He shook his head, as he'd seen cats who'd caught a mouse do. Something snapped in Ma'el's spine. Ma'el screamed in pain, then shouted out words that were obviously meant to dissolve the kraken spell. But Corwin had complete control of the kraken shape now, and the words had no effect.

Corwin felt the world lurch around him, a feeling similar to the one he'd had during the passage through the unis. Ma'el was trying to bend space around them, but Corwin didn't know why. He flung Ma'el back onto the stone and flowed over him, allowing the little creatures that made up the kraken to eat away at the evil mermyd, especially at the oculae that were the source of Ma'el's power.

Ma'el shrieked, and the folding of the unis vanished. Ma'el and the Corwin/kraken dropped together into the pool surrounding the stone platform. Then Corwin remembered that in water mermyds were much stronger—Ma'el had wanted to return to water. The Corwin/kraken coiled himself around Ma'el, who was rapidly healing, and threw him back onto the stone platform.

With every moment, Ma'el's power was returning. It was time for the final blow. Following Nia's advice, Corwin knew he had to do to Ma'el what he'd done to the kraken.

Corwin pulled at the life energy within Ma'el. Whatever power Ma'el spent to heal himself, Corwin absorbed. This wasn't like the wild lightning he'd received from Nia. This was like swallowing the sun. All of the oculae beneath Ma'el's skin resisted Corwin's pull. But Corwin was bigger now, in kraken form. Corwin could now contain as much energy as needed, because a kraken could expand its length as long as there was water to build from. And the shrine had an outlet to the sea.

Corwin felt himself swell, felt himself burn as if he were made of fire. The kraken shape was growing and growing, but Corwin couldn't stop. He could feel Ma'el's attempts to defend himself with the shreds of magic the mermyd and his oculae had left, but he was past a point of return. Corwin's power grew and grew, and pulled out Ma'el's energy faster and faster, until the life force in the mermyd dwindled and faded. Corwin didn't hold back, as Nia had instructed, and there was no sword to soften the damage done to Ma'el. Corwin drained every bit of the mermyd's life force until he knew, without a doubt, that Ma'el was dead and could never be revived.

But the roiling power was still within him—or actually,

Corwin was within it, helpless over what direction it might take. His mind expanded outward and knowledge flooded in, knowledge of the nature of time, the nature of life. Corwin found his consciousness floating in a vast darkness that was filled with pinpricks of light, each of them a sun. Corwin became frightened and sent a message to Gobaith. *Help! What do I do?*

He didn't receive the answer in words. Instead, a pattern pressed itself upon his mind, a ten-pointed star. Whirling symbols spun around the star, until they fell into a pattern that matched those carved on the stone.

Suddenly, the process began again in reverse. Corwin felt energy draining out of him, flowing into the floor of the chamber as if the very core of the Earth was taking the power from him. For several long moments, Corwin shook, helpless as his power receded. Corwin wondered if he was about to die the very same way he'd killed Ma'el.

And then, with a jolt, it stopped. Corwin was lying on his back on the round stone, in human shape again. There was a pile of ashes and bits of bone next to him, and Corwin realized with a shudder that it was the remains of Ma'el.

Corwin sat up. The symbols in the circle around the star he was sitting in still glowed, but they were fading. *All of my energy, and Ma'el's, was taken into the center of power*, Corwin thought. There was a deep rumble, and the stone beneath him quaked. A light rain of dust fell from the domed ceiling.

What if the energy it absorbed was more than this shrine was made to handle? Corwin wondered. *What if it collapses? Nia. I've got to get her out of here.*

Corwin stood and dove off the stone into the surrounding pool. He felt strong, healthier than he'd ever been in his life. He also felt like he'd retained some of the mysteries he'd learned, though it would take some time, maybe years, to sort them all out. But right now, Corwin's main concern was finding Nia again and escaping the shrine.

Corwin swam into the room that was all water and found Nia precisely where he'd left her. Henwyneb was bending over her, holding her hand, frowning in concern.

"Corwin! There you are! I found our lady of Atlantis here. I was afraid the worst had happened to you."

"Is she still alive?" Corwin asked, feeling as if his entire being rested on the answer.

"Yes, but barely."

Corwin let out a deep breath, then pulled himself out of the water and stood in the passageway. "We've got to get out of here," he said.

The shrine trembled again, harder this time, as if to emphasize his point.

"Take the sword," Corwin went on, "and I'll carry Nia."

Henwyneb took Eikis Calli Werr and Corwin scooped Nia up in his arms. Corwin noted that Henwyneb had wedged his walking staff in the hole with the swinging stone, making it possible to run down the passageway without fear of being struck.

"That was clever," Corwin said.

"Not at all. I came in again, chasing Nag, and from a distance saw you two go through this corridor. If I were less of an old coward, I would have joined you sooner."

"'Coward' is the last word I'd use for you," Corwin said as they moved on.

The next chamber was difficult. All the side stones on which he and Nia had run on upon their entry had fallen down. The stones in the middle were at different heights. And Corwin was carrying a heavy weight.

Corwin leaped over the rim rocks onto the square stones in the central circle. To his amazement, they held. "Come on!" he yelled to Henwyneb, then ran.

The shrine shuddered again, harder this time, and Corwin knew for sure that the walls and ceiling were going to come down. He stumbled and nearly fell on top of Nia, but he caught himself and ran on. At the far edge, at the doorway, Corwin had to lean precariously over the moat created when the rim rocks had dropped. Carefully, despite the little stones now raining down from this chamber's dome, Corwin slid Nia onto the floor of the corridor and leaped in after her. "Hurry, Henwyneb!"

The old man was still picking his way over the stones. As he got to the edge, he handed Corwin the sword hilt first. Henwyneb prepared to jump, but the shrine shook again and, with a cry of dismay, he fell forward over the gap.

Corwin lay down on the stone floor of the passageway and grabbed Henwyneb's right arm as the rest of the chamber paving-stones fell away. With all his strength, Corwin hauled Henwyneb up into the passageway beside him.

A low boom was heard in the distance, and a plume of dust puffed out of the doorway across the chamber.

"The third chamber's collapsed," Corwin said. "We have to run." Gathering Nia up again and slinging her over his shoulder, Corwin ran for all he was worth. The gravel scree ramp kept slipping under his feet. Another, louder rumble behind him indicated that the second chamber was collapsing.

Henwyneb was able to scramble out of the gravel-lined hole faster, aided by the sword—stabbing it into the dirt as an anchor. At the top, Henwyneb extended a hand to Corwin and helped pull him and Nia out onto the forest floor.

Just as Corwin got out, the first chamber collapsed with a soft *foomp* as the earth above it fell in, coating the three of them with a layer of dust.

Corwin laid Nia down on the soft moss and leaves of the forest floor while he caught his breath. She hadn't stirred the entire way during their escape. In sorrow and fear, Corwin placed his ear to her chest. There was a heartbeat, but it was faint. He put his face next to hers. "Nia?" he said softly. He put his hands over her hair and shut his eyes, trying to reach her with his mind. But there was nothing.

Corwin tried another way. *Gobaith! Can you hear me? Why can't I reach Nia?*

This time he received a response. *She has to use all of the strength she has left to keep herself alive. You must get her into water, quickly, or her effort will fail.*

Fighting back tears, Corwin turned to Henwyneb. "I have to get her into water, fast. Should I take her to the sea? What if she doesn't survive that long?"

"There's a small lake just to the south of here," Henwyneb answered. "The druids say its waters have healing powers. That's the closest and probably the best we can do for her, under the circumstances."

"The pond." Corwin remembered with a chill the strange fear he'd felt when he and Nia were last there. And how upset he'd been when Nia noticed it again on their way to the shrine. *Did I know this would happen somehow? Why couldn't I have stopped it?* But really, he wasn't sure what he could have done differently. The sword had shown them the path to victory and they'd taken it, even at the price of Nia's waking life. Sadly, Corwin picked Nia up once more and followed Henwyneb to the pond.

A faint mist was rising off the waters, just as it had been on that day when he'd first been here. Corwin remembered Nag playing along the pond's shores, and he was doubly sad.

He walked into the water, letting it soak his trousers and tunic. It was warmer than he expected and a thick, loamy, plant smell arose as he moved. A scent full of life. Corwin floated Nia upon the water and held his hand out to Henwyneb. "The sword, please," he said, his voice hoarse with sorrow.

Henwyneb handed him Eikis Calli Werr. Corwin placed the sword lengthwise along Nia's body and clasped her hands around the hilt. The area containing the oculus seemed to glow a little.

"Heal, Nia," Corwin said. "Heal and live, somehow. May whatever greater powers there are watch over you. I will wait for you." Corwin kissed her cool lips softly. Then he pushed her farther out into the lake.

She floated, for a time, her silvery hair fanned out in the water. She was beautiful in repose, as if the water were the most perfect bed for her long slumber. And then, slowly, she sank beneath the surface until he couldn't see a trace of her anymore.

Then Corwin wept. He let the sobs wrack his body and the tears flow from his eyes until they joined the water of the lake. In his mind, he heard Gobaith. *You've done all you can for her. Together, you saved Atlantis and the dry-land world as well. She will be remembered here as our greatest hero. And remember that she isn't dead, just resting deeply. There's always hope for the future.*

Corwin felt a hand on his shoulder. "Come away, Corwin," Henwyneb said. "There's nothing more we can do. Let's remember your lady as she was, brave and kind. Let her live in your heart and your thoughts."

Reluctantly, Corwin turned away and followed Henwyneb onto the lake shore. *What am I supposed to do now?* he wondered. For all the fear of the past few weeks, being joined with Nia and Gobaith and fighting Ma'el had given him a purpose. What came after that? Somehow he couldn't picture returning to the life of a beachcomber or petty thief.

Then the answer came to him, almost as if Nia *was* still in his thoughts. He would continue the Atlantean search for peace. He would pursue the ideal of a good king, unlike Vortigern or Ma'el. Someone who would preserve the world, not destroy it. He had no idea how he would achieve this, or even begin. But Corwin remembered the glory of the stars, the wisdom of the unis, and knew that some of the power of an Avatar still lay within him. He would find a way.

Epilogue

Year of Our Lord A.D. 475
Somewhere west of Carmarthen

The old man, with his long white beard and pointed, wide-brimmed hat, approached the lakeshore almost reverently. "You see, Majesty," he said to the blond man beside him. "Here is the lake, just as I've described it."

The king was a young man in his mid-twenties, but his face was worn and his muscles hardened from too many battles and too much worry. He frowned and looked out over the misty water. "I believe I've heard of this place. The mystics and druids call it a place of healing."

"So they do, Majesty, as they always have. It's larger than when I first came here, long ago. It was just a pond back then." The old man sighed, lost in memories.

"But the mystics and their myths didn't mention any swords," the king said, confused. "I don't understand why you said we'll find a replacement for my lost sword here. Unless there's a blacksmith hiding in these woods."

The old wizard smiled a knowing smile. "Oh, there are

hidden things here, Majesty, make no mistake."

The king regarded the old man with long-accustomed patience. "And will you reveal these things to me, old man, or will I have to pull the truth from you as I pulled my former sword from a stone?"

"Indulge me, Majesty. I've waited for this moment for a long time. Ever since I was a young man, younger than you, and had a different name. Once there was a lady, you see, who taught me many things. I learned most of my arts from her. She showed me how wide the world is, and how little I knew."

The king smiled. "She sounds like quite an extraordinary lady. I wish I could have met her."

"If you're the king I think you are, you will."

"How's that?"

"The lady sleeps here, within this lake. She's a nereid, a lady of the waters. She came to our land from beneath the sea. Her name is Niniane, and she was a hero to her people. She bears a sword that was forged long, long ago to be a gift to be given to a land-dwelling king who shows the promise of a peacemaker." More softly, the old wizard added, "I've waited all my life to see her again."

"And you're saying you think that I'm this king, the rightful bearer of the sword?"

"Let's wait and see, Majesty." The old man closed his eyes, deep in thought.

They didn't have to wait long. Presently, a shimmering shape appeared at the center of the lake. A beautiful girl with long, pale hair floated to the surface. She drifted closer and closer to the lakeshore, bearing a long, silvery sword upon her chest.

When she was within a few feet of the shore, the hilt of the sword she carried glowed a faint blue-green for a moment. Then her eyes opened. They were a bright aquamarine. She rolled over in the water and held out the sword, hilt first, to the astonished king.

The old wizard wiped a tear from his eye. "Ahh, there you are. She offers the sword to you. Take it, Arthur. Eikis Calli Werr is yours."

"Excaliwer? Excalibur?"

"Close enough," said Merlin.